Also by Frances O'Roark Dowell

Frances O'Roark Dowell

The Second Life of Abigail Walker

Atheneum Books for Young Readers
NEW YORK LONDON TORONTO SYDNEY NEW DELHI

ATHENEUM BOOKS FOR YOUNG READERS
An imprint of Simon & Schuster Children's Publishing Division
1230 Avenue of the Americas, New York, New York 10020

For information about special discounts for bulk purchases, please contact Simon &
Schuster Special Sales at 1-866-506-1949 or business@simonandschuster.com.
The Simon & Schuster Speakers Bureau can bring authors to your live event.
For more information or to book an event, contact the Simon & Schuster Speakers
Bureau at 1-866-248-3049 or visit our website at www.simonspeakers.com.
Book design by Sonia Chaghatzbanian
The text for this book is set in Horley Old Style
Manufactured in the United States of America
0712 FFG
First Edition
2 4 6 8 10 9 7 5 3 1
Library of Congress Cataloging-in-Publication Data
Dowell, Frances O'Roark.
The second life of Abigail Walker / Frances O'Roark Dowell. — 1st ed.
p. cm.
Summary: Bullied by two mean girls in her sixth-grade class, a lonely, plump girl
gains self-confidence and new friends after a mysterious fox gently bites her.
ISBN 978-1-4424-0593-6 (hardcover)
ISBN 978-1-4424-0595-0 (eBook)
[1. Self-confidence—Fiction. 2. Friendship—Fiction. 3. Overweight persons—Fiction.
4. Human-animal relationships—Fiction.] I. Title.
PZ7.D75455Sd 2012
[Fic]—dc23
2012010646

To Melvene Dowell,
with love

Be like the fox
who makes more tracks than necessary,
some in the wrong direction.
Practice resurrection.

—Wendell Berry
"Manifesto: The Mad Farmer Liberation Front"

Chapter One

the fox had been stepping into stories since the beginning of time. Important stories, everyday stories, stories that only mattered to one or two people. She sniffed stories out. When she smelled one that interested her, she closed her eyes and leaped into the air, moving through the invisible space between one story and the next. Sometimes she took chances and landed in unfortunate places. Like the story of the soldiers in the middle of desert, the sand seeded with explosives. A fox could get killed in a story like that.

Not that the fox ever got killed. She hadn't even managed to die of old age, although how old must she be? *Ancient of days,* her friend Crow liked to say when you asked him his age. The fox supposed that's how old she was too.

Now she stood at the edge of a field, in the invisible space between one story and another, and gazed across the green-goldness of it.

What had drawn her here?

This field, like all fields, had come from somewhere else. The birds had flown across its blank slate and dropped seeds into the waiting soil. The raccoons gathered burrs in their fur and deposited them as they tracked through the mud, and in the spring the earth took a deep breath, pulled forth roots, and sent out flowers and grasses.

There'd been something else here once, not too long ago. The fox could smell it. Something that had gone wrong. Her nose quivered. The scent was mixed: the something-gone-wrong smell, yes, but also mice and rabbits and the small berries that came at the beginning of fall, tiny, sour fruit she might eat just before the first frost. These were smells she remembered from the oldest stories, the laughing stories, stories where her kits gathered around her and chattered and barked.

Suddenly the heavy, dark smell of exhaust from the road filled the fox's snout. A bus? A truck? Soldiers back from Al Anbar? Quick, quick, burrow into the center of a clump of weeds. Something was coming. Someone. What would she witness this time?

Maybe it was someone who could help, she told herself, trying to stay calm. Maybe they've sent someone to help.

The fox trembled, and she waited.

Chapter Two

abby was trying to feel brave, but feeling brave was not something she was good at. In fact, she was chicken. A coward. A natural-born conflict avoider. And she was doomed. Whatever happened next, it would not be good, and her day, which had been completely rotten so far, would only get worse.

There was no way around it, though. She knew Kristen would hear about what happened in language arts. Myla was in Abby's class; so was Casey. They were part of Kristen and Georgia's group, and they'd tell faster than milk spilling from a knocked-over glass.

She wondered if Kristen would use it against her right away ("Hey, Tubby—oh, I'm just teasing! Take a joke!") or if she would bring it out later for maximum hurtage. Ever since Claudia had moved and Abby had taken refuge on the fringes of Kristen's group, she had learned how Kristen worked. Sometimes Abby was in with Kristen, sometimes she was out.

Mostly Abby was out, although she kept trying to find ways to be in. Sixth grade was no time to go off on your own, pretending like having friends didn't matter. So she offered Kristen her desserts, and some mornings she did Kristen's math homework on the bus. It didn't seem to make much of a difference, though.

Walking into the cafeteria, Abby wondered how much Myla and Casey would tell. Would they give Kristen the whole story or just the most embarrassing part? Oh, why hadn't Abby picked another word for her acrostic poem? Why not "rainbow" or "horse" or "volleyball"? Why, oh why, had she chosen "bathtub"?

"Bathtub? Hmm, sounds interesting," Mr. Lee

had said that morning, and he wrote the word "bathtub" on the board. "I've always liked the way the word 'tub' sounds, that 'ub' sound."

Marco Perry had been the one who started the chant. He'd slapped his hands on his desktop and called out, "Tubby! Chubby! Abby! Tubby! Chubby! Abby!"

Almost all the boys had joined in, except for Weber Logan, genius, who couldn't be bothered, and Anoop Chatterjee, a very serious and quiet boy who never joined in anything the other boys did.

"Quiet! Everyone!" Mr. Lee had called out, but it was no good. He was too new and too young. He didn't have control.

Abby had tried very hard not to cry. She did all the tricks. She stared straight ahead, breathed in deep through her nose, thought about her starfish collection.

But she'd made the same mistake she always made: She thought about her mom, and how upset she would be if she knew what was happening. Abby imagined her mom sitting at the kitchen table with her cup of coffee, reading one of the giant history books she loved so much. She was happy because her children were safely at school, and Abby's dad was in his office over the garage, and she had the house to herself and could read about Abigail Adams or George Washington or Thomas Jefferson and take notes for the class she taught on colonial America at the local college. At least thirty books were stacked around her reading chair in wobbly piles, and Abby's mom was always yelling, "Watch out for the books!" whenever anyone got too close.

If she knew boys in Abby's class were calling her names, her face would crumple up, and she would have to put away her books and her coffee, turn off the radio that played classical music all day in the kitchen.

Abby's mom couldn't stand very much unhappiness.

When Abby thought of her mother unhappy in her kitchen, the tears started to fall. Which only made things worse. Which only made the chanting boys chant more gleefully.

Abby resigned herself to crying. That was the

only way to make it stop. *The only way out is through,* her fifth-grade teacher, Mrs. Reisman, had liked to say. Sometimes you just had to cry until you were done crying. Finally a moment would come when you felt your eyes dry, and then you let out a little sigh. If you were sitting with a friend, you might smile to let her know the worst was over.

Do not think about Claudia, Abby told herself harshly.

But then she remembered that when she got home, she could e-mail Claudia or maybe even call her. She might say, *I bet you don't miss the boys in this school. They don't do anything but tease you and call you names.*

And Claudia would say, *Don't forget, we'll have our own apartment someday, and we won't let any mean people come visit us.*

The apartment. That was a good thought, and Abby tried to hang on to it. Once, in fourth grade, she and Claudia had taped together four shoeboxes and pretended they were the rooms of the apartment they planned to share one day. They cut doors in the side of the boxes, so you could get from the kitchen to the living room, the living room to the bedroom. Their real apartment would have hallways, of course, but it was okay that the shoe-box apartment just had doors.

Mr. Lee asked a tall, gangly boy named Martin to read his acrostic poem, and the boys' chanting wound down. Abby sniffed quietly and wished she had a tissue. She wished the girl who sat catty-corner from her would turn around and smile. But Abby had stopped crying, and it had only taken her a few minutes. That was good.

She opened her notebook to a blank page and began drawing the plans for her bedroom in the apartment. She sketched in twin beds and a mini-fridge. She drew a smaller bed for her dog, and then she drew a tiny quilt folded neatly on top of the dog's bed. She drew floral-patterned wallpaper and a giant flat-screen TV. She drew without stopping.

When the bell rang, Abby had blinked several times and shaken her head, surprised to find herself in Mr. Lee's classroom instead of her apartment, which seemed much more real to her, even if it only existed in her imagination. The other kids scurried out of the classroom. Only Anoop Chatterjee took his time, carefully inserting his notebook and pen into his backpack. When he saw Abby watching him, he smiled at her slightly and nodded.

Abby gave a weak smile back and stood up. She took in a big breath and let it out slowly, preparing herself for what she knew was coming.

She could have gone to the library instead of the cafeteria. Mrs. Longee, the librarian, liked her. She was recruiting her for Battle of the Books. Abby hadn't told her yet that she wasn't going to do it. She loved the idea of being on a team of kids who read for fun, but she was afraid she wouldn't read the books on the list. She had a bad habit of not reading books she was told to read. She liked to choose her own.

But she was hungry and she wanted chocolate milk with her sandwich, and she figured she might as well get it over with.

"I'm thinking about going on a diet," Kristen

announced as soon as Abby sat down at the table. "I'm getting so fat. My jeans are really tight."

Everyone rushed to assure Kristen she wasn't the least bit fat. Abby held back for a moment before joining in. She wanted to seem sincere. "You look great, Kristen. You're probably too thin, even."

Mistake. Kristen was *not* too thin. She was not too fat. She was just right, and to suggest otherwise—well, you just didn't do that.

"So, have your parents ever put you on a diet?" Kristen asked Abby, sounding concerned. "Because I've heard that one of the worst things you can do when you have an overweight child is to force her to diet. It's how girls get bulimic. Although, if you ask me, bulimia sounds like a great diet plan. Eat whatever you want! All you have to do is throw it up later."

The other girls giggled. Abby felt her cheeks grow hot. *I'm not even that fat!* she wanted to yell. And it was true. They'd been weighed two weeks ago in gym. Abby had weighed one hundred and five pounds. Kristen had weighed eighty-eight. So what? Seventeen pounds wasn't that much more.

Abby looked around at the six girls at the table. Kristen, Georgia, Rachel, Casey, Myla, and Bess. They all weighed around ninety. They were all medium girls. They were medium smart, medium good at sports, their families had a medium amount of money. Kristen was the most important, and Abby was the least. She knew to stay quiet most of the time. To keep her opinions to herself. She was doing her best to be the most medium of the medium girls so that no one would notice her.

Abby knew she needed to be careful. If she said the wrong thing now, that would be two strikes. Then she'd probably do something stupid on the bus and Kristen would say, "Strike three!" and give her that dead-fish-eye look that meant Abby was all the way on the outside again. Then she'd have to sit at the very end of the table at lunch while everyone gave her the silent treatment, depending on the occasional sympathetic glance from Bess or Casey to get her through the period.

Abby looked down at her sandwich. It was tuna on homemade wheat bread. Her mother put two more teaspoons of honey in her dough than the recipe called for, so the bread was a little extra sweet, but not too sweet. Abby's mother wanted her to be friends with Kristen and Georgia. Abby's mother wanted her to be happy.

This bread makes me happy, Abby thought. *Being friends with Kristen doesn't.*

"Well?" Kristen said in a voice that suggested she was ready for Abby to show her the proper respect so they all could get on with eating their lunches. "Don't you think throwing up is a way you could lose weight?"

Abby opened her mouth to give the answer that would satisfy Kristen. But different words, unexpected words, came out. "I think it sounds sick. Like something you would have to be mentally ill to do."

Everyone at the table grew very, very quiet. Georgia, who had been crumpling a chip bag, stopped mid-crumple.

Kristen smiled, unconcerned. "Well, I think

fat people are mentally ill. In fact, I read an article that said that."

"Or, like, emotionally stunted," Georgia added. "You know, nobody loves them, so they eat all the time."

Abby almost said, *Maybe.* She almost said, *I think I read that article too.* She almost said the sort of thing she always said, so no one would be mad at her. But she didn't. Instead she slowly put her sandwich back into her lunch bag. She stood up. Her legs felt shaky. The skin around her eyes and nose was cold, as though she'd just dipped her face in ice.

"What are you doing?" Kristen asked her. "Sit down."

Abby didn't reply. She thought that if she opened her mouth, she might throw up. *What's gotten into you?* she could hear her mom cry out. Abby wanted to cry back, *I don't know!*

She started walking toward the cafeteria exit. Something hit her in the back of the legs. When she looked down, she saw Georgia's crumpled chip bag.

Well, she thought, pushing open the door with her shoulder. *I guess that's that.*

And for the rest of the afternoon, until the last bell rang, little sparks of light flashed from her fingers. No one else could see them, but she could.

Chapter Three

riding the bus home that afternoon was an exercise in sitting very still while a swarm of bees hummed behind her ears. Kristen and Georgia were buzzing about Abby's turncoat behavior, how she was lucky they'd been her friends at all, and now nobody would be her friend, who would want to be friends with a fatty like Abby?

Abby squirmed uncomfortably in her seat. The girl next to her, a fifth grader named Sonya, scootched closer to the window, and Abby flushed, wishing she didn't take up so much space. She squeezed her thighs closer together, sat up straighter, sucked in her cheeks.

"Did you hear her say 'medium' when Mrs. Moser asked her what size shirt she needed for the chorus recital?" Kristen asked in a super-loud voice. "Medium! That's a joke! Extra large would be more like it."

Abby stared intently at the head of the boy in front of her. He had three cowlicks that she could see, and one was sticking straight up. Did he care? Did he stand in front of the mirror in the morning and rub hair gel on top of his head to try to make the cowlicks lie down? Did it bug him when someone asked him what size shirt he wore? Did he lie about being a medium, even when he knew he was really a large? Did he dread the day in PE when they got weighed like pumpkins at the state fair and everyone listened as hard as they could when the teacher told her assistant what numbers to write down in the record book?

Probably not. First of all, he was a boy, and Abby was pretty sure boys didn't care about stuff like hair and shirt sizes. She had two brothers, so she knew this from firsthand experience. And second, from what Abby could see, he was a regular-size kid. He probably didn't give it a second thought when they got weighed in PE. What would that be like, Abby wondered, not to care? To walk up to the scale, still joking around with your friends behind you, not noticing as the PE teacher fiddled with the marker, pushing it farther to the right, and then a little farther, the number getting higher and higher. She bet he didn't stand there with his eyes shut tight, his stomach churning, praying that he'd magically lost ten pounds overnight.

"I don't know why we started being friends with her in the first place," Kristen said from behind her. "What a waste of time."

"Are they talking about you?" Sonya whispered out of the side of her mouth, like she was an undercover agent in a movie.

Abby shook her head. "No, it's this girl in their homeroom they don't like," she whispered back.

"Named Abby?"

Abby nodded, and Sonya turned back to the window with a snort.

Okay, maybe walking away from Kristen's

table hadn't been such a great idea. Really, what had Abby been thinking about? She should have just said yes, throwing up was a way a person could lose weight. She should have said she was going on a diet that very afternoon.

A part of Abby was desperate to turn around and swear she'd only been joking. But she knew it was too late. She was tired of doing things and saying things just to make other people like her. She wanted to do and think what she felt like, even if nobody ever talked to her again. It was terrifying, but that's what she wanted.

Finally the bus pulled up to the corner of Ridge Valley Road. Abby scurried down the aisle and practically leaped out the door to the pavement. She needed to make a getaway.

She ran.

"Who are you running away from?" Kristen called after her. It sounded like a threat, but what kind of threat could it have been? Did she want to fight? Abby outweighed her by seventeen pounds, as Kristen had pointed out at least ten times on their ride home. If nothing else, Abby could squash her.

Her feet pounded down the hill toward her house. When she reached her front yard, she stopped. She didn't want to go inside. Her mother might have just made cookies. She was the kind of mother who did that kind of thing when she was home from work, baked treats thirty minutes before her children got home, so the house would smell warm and inviting when they walked through the front door.

She couldn't go into her sweet-smelling house with this pack of jumbled feelings—*I'm free! I'm doomed!*—on her back. Her mother would sense it. She'd want to smooth things out. But Abby didn't want smoothness. She wanted rough edges. She wanted to feel whatever it was she was feeling.

She stood for a moment in the yard across the street from her house. The jungle, her father called it. It was the strangest story. The summer before last, the people who'd lived there had gone to Japan for a year. They paid a man to mow the lawn, but nobody ever went into the house while they were gone to check on things. The roof sprang a leak, probably sometime right after the owners left the country, and when they returned a year later, the house was contaminated with toxic mold.

For two weeks in July, Abby and her brothers John and Gabe had watched from their front porch as men in white suits, with HAZMAT printed across the back, tore the house down, brick by brick, board by board. It was like watching a movie run backward. It might have sounded boring, but it was almost impossible not to look.

Really, it was like watching something die.

"I think you children ought to watch from inside the house," her mother had fretted nearly every morning when she found them sitting on the porch steps, licking dripping Popsicles as they peered across the street, still in their pajamas.

"They'd tell us if it was dangerous, Mom," John had insisted. "I think they sprayed everything before they started tearing it down."

When the men were done, nothing but the driveway was left to give a hint there'd been anything there other than a weedy patch of dirt.

All the neighbors had wondered what would happen next. Was the ground contaminated? Could another house be built on the same spot?

If the ground was contaminated, it didn't stop a million weeds from sprouting on the lot almost overnight. Wildflowers sprang up. Saplings took root. A flock of dandelions landed in what used to be the front yard and made itself at home. Abby's father threatened to go after them with a tank of weed killer, but he was too scared to get close enough. What if mold spores were still flying around?

Abby loved the new wild place across from her house. Every morning it seemed there was a new flower standing on a spindly leg, some yellow speckled bird that couldn't be from around here—but where else could it be from? In August she checked out a copy of the *National Geographic Field Guide to Birds of North America* from the library and began making a list. *Junco, oriole, hummingbird.*

The yard across the street was the opposite of her yard. Abby's mother was an indoor person. Her father worked eighteen hours a day. They paid a professional lawn service to keep the grass cut and the weeds down. In the late fall, a landscaper would come by to prune the azaleas and the boxwoods that guarded the front porch. Everything was symmetrical and neat. No wild things allowed.

Standing in the empty lot, Abby noticed the weeds were now up to her waist. What would be left at the end of the world? Some people said cockroaches, but her money was on the weeds. She wanted to walk through them, part them down the middle like a greeny-brown sea. But she didn't want ticks. Ticks, like the idea of leeches, made her shudder all the way down to her toes. Anything stuck to her skin and sucking her blood she found highly problematic.

So she didn't part the sea of weeds, but she did walk around the edges.

And that's when she met the fox.

She wasn't used to wild animals, unless you counted squirrels and rabbits, but they never made her hair stand on end. So when the small red fox suddenly appeared, its eyes searching her face, its delicate, pointed nose sniffing, sniffing,

Abby had to stop herself from screaming. She was already shaky, newly escaped as she was from her life as a medium girl. And now, this fox, this *creature*. Would it kill her? Go for her jugular?

The fox tilted its head to one side, as though wondering something. She—or he—was a small animal. Abby could have punted it across the lot. She had opposable thumbs, a highly developed cerebral cortex. She had the advantage here.

But not really.

Were foxes related to dogs? Abby racked her brain. They were, weren't they? So why did this fox remind her of a cat? *Sly as a fox*, she thought, and then she thought of her dog, Bingo, who was smart when he needed to be, smart enough to hide under the couch when they made signs they were going out and about to crate him, but not sly. Not crafty.

"Who are you?" Abby asked the fox. She squatted, held out her hand. Did she expect the fox to lick it? To rub its head against her fingers, hoping she'd scratch it behind the ears, the way Bingo would?

The fox came closer, eyes still on her. "Do you live here?" Abby asked.

Another step closer. Abby wasn't scared anymore. She couldn't believe how close the fox was getting. She held out her hand an inch from its snout. The fox opened its mouth. She thought the fox was yawning, she thought it might curl up at her feet and nap. And then its teeth came down on her hand. Lightly. As if to barely break the skin.

Abby fell back, landed on her bottom, and watched the fox scurry off into the sea of weeds. The fox had bitten her! Her left hand began to tingle, and she examined the two small puncture wounds. Two tiny pearls of blood had risen on the skin. She knew she should wipe the blood away; if her mother saw it, she'd ask questions, rush her to the emergency room, have her stomach pumped, her appendix removed. She would forbid Abby to ever return to the empty lot.

She wiped her hand on her jeans, then spit on it and rubbed the spit so that nothing was left to see except for two small dots. *Fox dots*, she thought, feeling oddly giddy.

Abby's mother, reading in the living room, only called "Hello" when she heard Abby's footsteps in the hall, too involved in the lives of colonial America to give Abby her full frontal welcome. Once in her room, Abby flung her backpack onto her bed and opened her closet. She walked in and closed the door behind her.

She always did her best thinking in her closet. When she was younger, she'd pretended her bedroom closet was her house. She drew pictures and hung them on the wall: a deliriously happy yellow daisy that towered over a pink cottage; a portrait of the sisters in *Little Women*, all in hoop skirts, like they'd gone to visit Scarlett O'Hara in *Gone with the Wind*. She tucked away snacks in shoe boxes. And candy, of course. Always candy.

Abby had a secret candy life. The summer after fourth grade, when her father had told her mother to put her on a diet, she'd started hiding Kit Kat bars she bought at the pool snack bar in the pockets of her bathrobe and the navy blazer that her mother bought for her at a consignment shop, thinking it might look cute with jeans, and which Abby had never worn. After a day where her food choices had been low-fat yogurt, four-ounce chicken breasts, and Special K with skim milk, she slipped into her closet and dipped into her stash of chocolate.

"She should be losing weight faster than this," her father would tell her mother after Abby's Saturday morning weigh-ins. "You're not letting her snack, are you?"

"People lose at different rates," her mom would say, looking at Abby with a worried expression. Was there something wrong? Thyroid problems, maybe?

Abby would shrug. "Maybe I should exercise more."

"We should all go bike riding!" her mother would exclaim, and her father would grunt—not a yes, not a no, more of a *Get real*. In order to go bike riding you had to have free time. Abby's father had none. Wanted none was maybe more to the point.

Sitting in her closet now, she could feel her hand throbbing slightly. Could the fox have been rabid? Maybe she should tell her mom about the bite. She didn't want her arm to fall off, after all; she had enough problems without losing an arm. But that fox hadn't been foaming at the mouth, hadn't acted crazy. *Crazy like a fox.* Abby wondered what that meant. Well, she knew what it meant, sort of. Sometimes a person might act crazy to throw you off what they were really up to. Did foxes do that? They must, or why have the saying?

After half an hour or so, the tingling stopped. Her mom called from downstairs that dinner was almost ready. Abby wondered if she would tell her about Kristen, how they weren't friends anymore. She wanted to, but she knew she probably wouldn't. Still, to be able to say, *I am not friends with Kristen Gorzca*, to make that declaration, it would have been like opening a door. *Please come in*, Abby would say to her mom. *Meet the original Abigail Walker, a girl who does and says what she wants when she wants to.*

She stood, opened the closet door, and emerged. She looked at her hand. The marks were gone. She held out her arms, examined them, looked at her legs, patted her belly. All her parts looked and felt exactly as they had when she woke up that morning.

But she was pretty sure she had become an entirely different person.

Chapter Four

poets throughout

the ages could not keep their pens off her sleek red fur, her thin, elegant nose. The fox reminded herself of this as she stood beside a chicken coop the next morning, contemplating an especially plump bird. She was too grand for this sort of thing—how common to rob a chicken coop! Leave the chickens to the raccoons, whom the poets had largely ignored and for good reason.

Besides, enough carnage! Enough bones and blood, enough feathers flying without bodies to lift into the air.

The fox moved away from the coop, which was in the middle of an ordinary backyard, not far from the field where she'd met the girl. She was taking the morning to explore the neighborhood, the green-turning-to-gold-and-brown neighborhood. She needed to look for traps, check the perimeters. It was, aside from the chicken coop and the empty field in the middle of all those houses, a run-of-the-mill kind of place. The houses were nice, but not mansions, and the yards were indistinguishable from one another. Boxwoods and broom shrubs, pyracantha. Mulch to keep down the weeds.

The fox appreciated neighborhoods like this. If she kept her head down, no one bothered her, because no one was looking for her, and she was free to explore. For the most part, people stayed inside their houses, and when they came out, it was to get into their cars and drive somewhere else. They never thought about animals other than their own dogs and cats. Had no idea that their backyards and the woods were teeming with snakes and woodchucks, raccoons (horrible creatures) and mice and moles and voles. They would never guess in a million years that a fox was in their midst.

On those mornings she desired attention, all the fox had to do was stand beneath a kitchen window. Sooner or later someone would look out, and then there would be a cluster of faces, fingers pointing, some oohing and aahing, an occasional scream. However people felt about her, her mere presence thrilled them.

Of course.

Taking a last, backward glance at the chickens, the fox slipped into the thin woods behind the coop and trotted in the direction of the girl's house. The girl in the field. The fox had been careful to be gentle. All she had wanted to do was say, *I'm here. I'm in your story now, and you're in mine. Let's see what happens next.*

That was the interesting part. You entered a story drawn by a scent, a rumor, a promising circumstance, and then you waited to see what came next. What came next for the boy in the covered wagon holding his baby brother and singing lullabies? For the president in his tall hat, sitting in his theater box, enjoying the play? What came next for the girl standing in the ocean of weeds, who held out her hand to the fox as though welcoming a friend?

What came next for the fox?

Back to the field, she thought, looking both ways before she crossed the road. Maybe she'd find a mouse scurrying in between the chickweed and the thistles.

One little mouse, she told herself. *Where's the harm in that?*

Chapter Five

the next morning Abby strolled up the hill to the bus stop, a book about artists who painted flowers in her hand. It was part of an Art for Young People series that had been her mom's when she was a girl. All of her mom's childhood books and college textbooks were stored in the basement, and sometimes Abby liked to look through them and wonder what her mom was like before she became the sort of person who worried all the time.

When her mom was nine, her older sister had died of leukemia. "That's all I remember from my childhood," she told Abby once. "Wendy sick, Wendy dying, Wendy dead. That's all there was."

It was strange, Abby thought, that she had an aunt she'd never known. Aunt Wendy. Whenever she thought of Wendy, she pictured a grown woman like her mother, only Wendy had never grown up. She'd died when she was twelve. Abby would be twelve in April, and sometimes lying in bed at night she got a spooky, sad feeling as she imagined dying of leukemia before she even had a chance to be a teenager. Who would come to her funeral? What would they say about her? She imagined boys like Jay Franks and Reid Windersole telling everyone how much they'd secretly liked her, how she was really the nicest girl they knew, much nicer than popular Lily Sanderson and Hollis Holman.

Sometimes when Abby read her mother's old books she tried to imagine one of her brothers dying, but it was impossible. Last year John had run through the patio door trying to catch a football. The glass had shattered around him in huge shards, but he'd hardly even been scratched. And Gabe was always covered in scabs, but if

Abby asked him did that cut hurt or that scrape, he just rolled his eyes. "I'm too tough to feel pain," he'd say, which always cracked Abby up. Gabe was eight and wanted to be a hockey player when he grew up, even though he'd never ice-skated in his life. He just thought it was cool how hockey players were always beating up on each other and never getting in trouble for it.

Abby was happy to be walking up the hill, reading a book about art and flowers and think-ing about her brothers. She was happy that she didn't have to worry if this was going to be a good Kristen day or a bad Kristen day. She was happy because she'd found a Kit Kat bar she'd forgotten about in her scrap paper drawer and snuck it into her lunch bag. Now that she wasn't going to sit with the medium girls, she could have what she wanted. No one would be there making snarky faces as they checked out what she had to eat.

When she got to the top of the hill, she glanced up from a painting of a sunflower so yel-low that it practically glowed in the dark and saw Kristen and Georgia. When they saw her, they turned away. Abby's stomach went icy cold, and then her skin got prickly hot because it infuriated her that they could make her feel scared and alone just by turning around. They weren't the boss of her feelings! But a second later she thought maybe they were, because she suddenly wanted to change back to being someone who tried to get along with everyone else. She could beg. Or she could laugh. *What a good joke! I can't believe you took me seriously.*

Did her hand throb a little? She thought maybe it did, and she remembered the little red fox with its delicate nose and intelligent eyes. She hadn't been scared of the fox, so why was she scared of Kristen and Georgia? She thought about how gently the fox had bitten her. It could have been so much worse! A fox could snap a chicken's neck with its mouth if it wanted to. So maybe the fox was trying to tell her something by biting her. Maybe biting her was its crafty and sly way of getting her attention.

Abby stood at the edge of the bus stop and kept thinking about the fox and what it had been trying to tell her. What could a fox know about her? Had the fox been sneaking around the edges of her life for a while now, noticing things, coming up with ideas to make Abby's life better? Did the fox have some clever, foxy advice for what she should do about Kristen and Georgia?

Even when the bus came lumbering down the road, Kristen and Georgia kept their backs to Abby. She started to giggle. There was something funny about how dramatic they were being, like actors in a movie about girls who didn't like each other anymore. She had to hand it to Kristen, though. A lesser girl would have swung around and snapped at her—*Oh, you think you're so smart, so funny, so great*—but not Kristen. Abby could see Georgia twitch. Georgia wanted to turn around and slap her. But Kristen put her hand on Georgia's shoulder, and they stayed frozen in place.

Abby got on the bus first. She took the seat behind the bus driver and returned to her book on art and flowers. One of the artists had been able to draw anything in the world from the time he was five years old, and people from miles around came to look at his pictures. When Abby was five, she'd built a Lego village under her bed and dreamed that one day she would be tiny enough to live in it.

Kids filed by. One kid, the next kid, the next kid, the next, then Georgia, who stopped at Abby's seat and leaned down to whisper in her ear. "You're dead," she hissed, and Abby felt confused. Really? Kristen and Georgia were going to kill her? Were going to have her killed?

She blew into her fist. Her breath was warm. She wasn't dead, and she probably wasn't going to be dead anytime soon.

"Okay," Abby replied to Georgia. "That's fine."

Mr. Lee was sitting at his desk when she walked into language arts, but when he saw her he stood and came over to her desk. Watched Abby wrestle her LA notebook from her backpack.

"You doing okay?" he asked quietly.

Abby wished he would just forget about what had happened in class yesterday. She was a different person now. Didn't he know that?

"I'm fine," she told him. "Everything's fine."

When Myla and Casey walked into the classroom, Abby smiled at them to see what would happen, and wasn't surprised when they acted like they hadn't seen her. She blew into her fist again. She still wasn't dead.

Don't get cute, her father liked to tell her, and Abby heard him say it again as she waved good-bye to Myla and called, "See you later, Casey," at the end of the period.

Who was being cute?

She crammed her books back into her backpack. She had PE next, and it was a dress-out week. She wondered if the bleachers would be pulled out from the wall in the gym. If they were, she might be able to hide underneath them, the linoleum cool beneath her legs. She wouldn't have to spend the entire period pulling her shirt so it stretched enough to hide the tops of her legs in the stupid gym shorts that made her feel practically naked. Most sixth-grade girls had toothpick legs, skinny bird legs, but not Abby. She had Jell-O knees, marshmallow thighs. It was humiliating.

A shadow fell across her desk. When Abby

looked up, Anoop Chatterjee was standing in front of her. He was such a skinny, slim-jim kind of kid, she was surprised he cast a shadow at all.

"I am correct that you have B lunch?" he asked, and when she nodded, he said, "Would you care to join me?"

If Anoop Chatterjee had asked her to marry him, she couldn't have been any more surprised. "Uh, where do you sit?"

"With my friend Jafar, near the teachers' table. But Jafar is not here today, and I would like company."

He didn't appear to be nervous. He didn't appear to be madly in love with her. He looked at Abby in a calm and measured way, as though he was willing to wait many minutes for her answer.

"Sure, okay," she told him. "That would be nice."

He gave a slight nod of his head. "Yes. I believe so."

So she could do what she wanted to do, she thought as she trudged along C hallway to PE. Could eat lunch with Anoop Chatterjee. Could say yes. How funny. How strange. She looked around her. People banged closed their lockers and yelled across the corridor and shoved into each other and laughed in loud barks. They weren't paying any attention to her. They weren't checking out her socks to see if they matched her shirt or whispering about her behind their cupped hands. They had their lives, she had hers.

That was all she was asking for.

Chapter Six

WE DO not know each other very well," Anoop said when they'd taken their lunches out and begun to eat. "You may ask me a question about myself if you wish."

Abby bit off a piece of her Kit Kat bar, which she was treating as an appetizer. She tried to come up with the most interesting question she could think of. "Are you a Hindu?"

"No, the people in my family are scientists, not Hindus," Anoop told her. "My parents are completely rational. They think God is a nice idea, but an unlikely one. My sister goes to

Catholic school, though, and she quite enjoys the mandatory services. She says it is very calming when the priest says the Eucharist. But she will not become a Catholic herself. My parents would disown her."

"Does she want to become a Catholic?"

Anoop gave Abby an odd look. "No, of course not. Why would she?"

She shrugged. "No reason, I guess." She pointed to what looked like a rolled-up tortilla poking out of his lunch bag. "What's that?" It felt rude to ask, but she was interested. She was used to medium-girl lunches, containers of pink yogurt, turkey and Swiss cheese sandwiches on honey-wheat bread. Lunchables.

"That is a *dosa*," Anoop informed her. "A kind of pancake. But it is made with rice and lentils instead of flour. Inside, chutney. My grandmother gives this to me almost every day. I have asked her for something else, but it makes her cry. She is very devoted to *dosas* with coconut chutney."

He eyed Abby's turkey sandwich. "This is like what Jafar brings," he said, pointing at it. "His grandmother doesn't live with him."

After that, they were quiet. It was a nice quiet. Abby didn't feel nervous, like she should make conversation, ask Anoop about the other items in his lunch. When both of them were finished eating, Anoop smiled at her and asked, "Shall we walk? We can see if any of the fellows are playing at the field."

They walked to the farthest playing field, the one that was always soggy around the edges, near the fence. A brown-skinned boy with a mop of black hair falling into his eyes called out when he saw them. "Anoop! Did you bring your soccer ball? Thomas just kicked ours over the fence!"

Anoop held out his empty hands. "No, I left it at home. I had to bring in my rocket booster for science club today, and I didn't have room for anything else."

The boy smiled a charming smile. A smile meant to woo. "Would you care to climb the fence to retrieve the one we lost?"

"I don't have the right shoes," Anoop informed him, pointing to his soft leather loafers. "These would get torn. Besides, Thomas, it is against the rules."

"It's not like we're trying to escape," the boy pointed out. "We just want our ball back."

Abby eyed the fence. Could she do it? The day before, she'd have said, no way, never. But maybe today was different?

They'd had rock climbing in PE two weeks before, but when it was Abby's turn, she'd slipped and slid and scrambled up three feet of wall before falling. She'd refused to try a second time.

"Come on, Abby, you can do it!" Coach Horton had called from where she stood under the basketball hoop, a clipboard in her hand. "Don't give up!"

Abby had just shaken her head and walked over to the bleachers. She was tired of being Coach Horton's pet project. "We're going to get you in shape!" the PE teacher had declared at the beginning of the year, and she'd pounded Abby for three weeks with encouragement and positive feedback.

Maybe if they'd started out the year with something other than gymnastics. Abby was famous for not being able to do a cartwheel. The most she could accomplish was a halfhearted roundoff. Even Cornelia Kidd, with her stick arms and skim-milk skin, the tiny vein you could see pulsing in her forehead whenever she was nervous, even Cornelia Kidd could do a cartwheel.

But Abby failed cartwheels and handstands. She sprinted toward the vault and then veered off at the last second. "You can *do* it, Abby!" Coach Horton would cry, but by the time they got to the uneven parallel bars and Abby couldn't hold on for more than ten seconds no matter how much chalk she put on her hands, Coach Horton had more or less admitted defeat.

After Abby refused to try climbing the rock wall a second time, Coach Horton had walked over to the bleachers and sat down next to her. "You could climb that wall, you know. It just takes practice. Everything just takes practice."

"I don't have any muscles," Abby told her, leaning forward so that her nose was almost touching her knee. "I mean, look. I'm totally floppy."

Coach Horton shook her head. "You're totally

flexible. And you do have muscles. You just don't have confidence."

"You're right," Abby agreed. "I don't."

"Here, take this," Coach Horton said, handing Abby her clipboard. "Why don't you be my helper for a while? And maybe you could come to the gym during recess, when nobody's in here, and practice a little bit?"

"Okay," Abby had told her, taking the clipboard. But when she'd gone by the gym the next day, some boys were already there playing basketball, and Abby decided she didn't really care that much about climbing walls after all.

Looking at the fence now, Abby thought of how it should be climbed. If you started with a running jump, you could hit it more than halfway up and would only have two more feet to go, she figured. If you could avoid the barbs at the top of the fence, you could plant your hands on the bar and pull yourself up, launch yourself over.

Like you could do that, she heard Kristen's voice say. *Yeah, right. Like, maybe if there was an escalator leading up to the top.*

Abby's hand suddenly throbbed where the fox had bitten her.

"I'll try it," she told Anoop and Thomas. "I don't know if I can do it, but I'm wearing sneakers at least."

The boys—there were seven in all, including Anoop, all of them skinny and scrawny or fleshy and round, tall for their age, short for their age, pale skinned, brown skinned, unmuscled— cheered Abby on as she ran toward the fence and flung herself at it. She grasped for a chain link, held on, poked the toe of her left foot into another link, pulled herself up.

A fleeting thought: Were they looking at her butt? Were they thinking that it was big?

Maybe they were, she didn't know. But they cheered and they whistled. One boy yelled, "Way to go, Annabelle!" and Anoop snapped, "It's Abigail, you idiot!"

She felt for the top bar with her hand and made contact with a barb. It didn't hurt, but promised worse if she applied more pressure. She moved her hand, groped for a better spot. Mid-grope, her arms gave out on her. Abby tried

49

to hug the fence, but it was no good. She toppled to the ground.

Several of the boys rushed over to her, patted her on the back, asked if she was okay. "You almost had it!" one of them exclaimed, and the others agreed.

A small boy named Max Ortega, a sixth grader who rode Abby's bus, stepped forward. "I think I can do it. I think Abby had the right idea. You have to make a running start."

They all stood back and watched as Max Ortega sprinted toward the fence and landed two-thirds of the way up. In no time he was over and on the other side. "Now, where's the ball?" he called to them in a cheerful voice. "Help me find it before somebody's pit bull comes after me."

The ball was found, the game started over. Abby played goalie for Anoop's team and blocked three shots. The first one she blocked by accident, putting her hands in front of her face so the ball wouldn't hit her nose. But the second time she actually ran toward the ball and scooped it up.

"You've got the hang of it, Abigail!" Thomas shouted. "Excellent!"

"Jafar will be in school tomorrow," Anoop told her as they walked back to the building for fifth period. "But I'm sure he wouldn't mind it if you joined us for lunch."

"Thank you," Abby said. She brushed some dirt off her jeans. "I'd like that."

Anoop bowed slightly. "Yes," he said. "I very much agree."

Chapter Seven

the tiniest sounds caused her to jump. Birds alighting on branches, squirrels rustling through piles of leaves in search of their stashes. *What, what, what.* The fox panicked, heart racing, head throbbing. *Who's there? What's happening?*

The fox reminded herself that wherever she went, there was no avoiding the crack of a stick, a muffler's backfire, a blue jay quarreling with its mate. City or country, noises popped up from nowhere. No need to run for her life every time an acorn hit the tin roof of a backyard shed.

She calmed herself with mantras. *No sand here*, she'd tell herself, digging into the red clay dirt beneath her paw. No soldiers, no bombs, no trucks barreling toward the sandbags, no explosions thundering across the desert.

No. She was in her field. Flowers and tall grasses waved in the breeze, scattering seeds. Birds sang in the trees. And the girl. She belonged to the field too. The fox liked the girl, liked how her reddish-brown hair was as pretty as a wren's wing in the late afternoon sun, liked how she'd crouched down and tenderly reached out her hand. Who was tender to a fox? Other hands had taken aim at her, had been raised against her in fear, but not the girl's. The night before, waking from a nightmare, the fox thought of the girl, and her heart fell back into place.

The nightmare. It was the same nightmare she had every night. The soldiers stood outside the building—the soldiers who had looked like boys to her, six of them, laughing, cutting up, two of them acting out some scene from the night before. The fox had only just stepped into the story, drawn by the scent of sun on sand, the succulent desert flowers, and the sound of young men laughing. She was sitting in the front seat of a Jeep, listening to the soldiers' stories, when a truck came barreling through the gate, picked up speed, and crashed through sandbags. And then the fox was watching from the air—she was flying through flames!—and there was a soldier flying with her, they were flying together, and then the soldier disappeared, and the fox was falling, falling, picking up speed, she was about to explode against the ground—

The fox always woke up before she hit. But even as her eyes opened to the world around her, the world that was now this field and its flowers and weeds and birds, she could still hear the thundering.

No sand here, she told herself. And the soldier? Still flying, maybe. That was the most she could hope for.

Chapter Eight

abby's plan was to spend most of Saturday in the yard across the street, drawing plans for the houses she might live in one day and thinking about things. She wanted to think about Anoop and why he had asked her to eat lunch with him. She wanted to think about the fox's bite, how it might have changed her. She felt different, though when she looked at herself in the mirror after her shower, she still looked exactly the same, with her doughy stomach and moon-round face.

She'd dragged a beach chair behind a wide oak

so that she couldn't be seen from the road, and placed a cooler filled with bottled water, her drawing pad and pencils, and frozen red grapes beside it. She liked how grapes tasted sweeter when you froze them, more like candy. If the fox showed up, she'd offer it one, or the whole bunch, if that's what the fox wanted. She'd promise the fox that the grapes weren't sour, the way they were in the Aesop fable. She would never give *her* fox sour grapes.

Abby sat down and studied the weeds around her. No one had planted them, no one stopped by and doused them with fertilizer, but here they were, growing like crazy. To Abby, the weeds looked triumphant. There had been a house here once, and now there was a .35-acre field of Queen Anne's lace and milkweed and tall grasses that Abby liked to imagine whispering, *We win, we win* when she walked past.

She looked at a weed with five purple petals. Why wasn't it considered a flower? Abby knew if her mom saw it in their yard, she'd pluck it out straightaway. This particular weed did look sort of sloppy, Abby supposed, and maybe flowers had to be neat and even. Still, who got to decide these things? Who got to point at plants and say, *You belong in a beautiful garden, and you deserve to be pulled up by the roots and chucked in the yard-waste bin?*

Abby popped a grape in her mouth and wondered if the people who bought this lot would mow all the weeds down. She frowned, already knowing the answer. If *she* bought the lot, she'd make a garden out of the weeds. She'd give them all beautiful names she made up, like *lapizuras azula*, and put a pretty fence around them. And then she'd build a house that looked just right surrounded by weeds.

What kind of house would that be, though? Abby pulled her drawing pad out of the cooler and set it on her lap. A tree house might be right for a yard full of weeds, only all the trees on this lot were at the edges. Could you have a tree house that stretched all the way across the yard, a tree house the size of a regular house? How would you get electricity to it? Abby definitely wanted electricity so she could watch TV and turn on lights at night.

Maybe another kind of house, then, one built lower to the ground. Maybe a cabin with a hole built right in the center of the floor so that the weeds could grow inside. She squinted her eyes, imagining, and started to draw.

After lunch, Abby brought three chocolate chip cookies wrapped in a paper napkin back to the chair with her, and the *Field Guide to Birds of North America*, which she had now renewed three times, in case any new species had flown into the yard at the tail end of summer. She'd been staring intently at a small, black bird with a red head and yellow eyes when she heard Kristen's voice coming over the tops of the weeds.

"We both have to knock on the door," Kristen said. "It would look weird if you were standing out here in the road."

"But what if her mom answers the door?" Georgia's voice replied. "How am I supposed to act all friendly and nice when basically I think her daughter is a piece of dirt?"

"All you have to do is stand there," Kristen insisted. "I'll do the talking."

Abby heard them crossing the road to her house. She heard the sound of gravel crunching under shoes. She heard the sound of feet stomping up her front steps. She ducked low in her chair, just in case they looked across the street. She was hidden behind a tree, but Kristen was the sort of person who could sniff out a hiding place in no time flat.

The question was, who would answer the front door? Her father was working, and her mother had gone to meet her friend Mary Katherine for lunch. If Gabe answered, he'd yell Abby's name up the stairs a couple of times, then shrug at Kristen and Georgia when she didn't yell back. If they asked him where he thought she was, he'd shrug again and close the door.

But if John answered the door, he might try to be helpful. John had always been nice to Claudia when she came over, unless he was with his friends. When he was with his friends, he seemed to feel like he had to roll his eyes a lot and call Abby and Claudia twerps and dweebs and ask them why they didn't have boyfriends yet. On his own, he was friendly as long as they didn't go into his room.

After John called around for Abby, he might offer suggestions. Had they checked over at Mrs. Vann's house? Sometimes on Saturdays Abby helped her sort her recycling. Or—and here he might look across the street and think for a moment—he'd seen her wandering around over there every once in a while. Maybe she was reading behind one of those trees.

The only thing Abby knew for sure was that she couldn't let them find her, even though she was probably just putting it off. Sooner or later they'd back her into a corner and—well, she didn't know what they'd do. She was dead, Georgia had said, and even though Abby knew that was only a figure of speech, still, a group of girls could kill you in their way. They could text evil rumors about you and make everyone stop talking to you, as though you didn't even exist. Abby had heard the stories.

She quickly folded her beach chair and stuffed the field guide and her sketchbook and pencils into the cooler. The back of the lot ran up against a low wooden fence, one that a five-year-old could climb. She leaned her chair against a post—she could pick it up later—and dropped the cooler on the other side. No one would think anything of an abandoned beach chair, but she thought the cooler might look suspicious.

Abby climbed over the fence easily and hopped to the ground. Picking up the cooler, she wound her way through a stand of trees to the edge of the next yard, hoping no one would be outside. When she got to the driveway, she saw a man over by some rosebushes with a sprayer, but his back was turned to her. She quickly made her way to the street.

The street was called Blue Valley Lane. Even though her bus picked up kids here, she really didn't know any of them. She didn't know how long the street was. Did it run parallel to Ridge Valley Road, or did it start to curve off in some other, completely different direction?

Maybe Blue Valley Lane emptied out into some interesting place she'd never heard about, a shopping center with an ice cream parlor, or a pond next to a tree where she could look for new birds. She turned right and began to hike along the sidewalk.

After she'd been walking for a few minutes, she noticed that a dog was following her. At first she made friendly noises at it, *hey, boy, good boy*, but it didn't come any closer. It stayed about ten feet behind her. She guessed it was some kind of hound; it had long ears and a brown nose and was speckled black and red, with freckles across its face.

The dog wasn't friendly or unfriendly. It was just there, and after a while Abby forgot about it and started looking around. The houses on Blue Valley Lane looked pretty much like the ones on Ridge Valley Road. They all seemed to be half house, half garage, and most of the houses were close to the street, so there was more backyard than front.

Abby glanced at the dog again, and that's when she saw Kristen and Georgia riding their bikes down the street in her direction. They were still about two blocks away. Abby didn't think they'd seen her yet, but her knees got wobbly anyway.

I've got to get out of here, she thought, and looked wildly around, in case there was an obvious bush to jump under or a car to duck behind.

The dog seemed unconcerned. Without any ado, he trotted across the street and scampered down a driveway. Abby decided to follow him. Maybe this was where he lived. Maybe his owners would come to the door and invite Abby inside for a drink of water. She wasn't supposed to go into strangers' houses, but it had to be safer than letting Kristen and Georgia catch up with her.

But the dog didn't go to the house. Instead he led Abby to a steep hill at the end of the driveway. Abby crashed down after him into the woods, the cooler smashing into her leg with each stride. The air turned cool as soon as they crossed into the deep shade, and Abby could hear running water. She followed the dog for another fifty yards, and there it was, a creek.

And on the other side of the creek, a boy.

Chapter Nine

how do you know Wallace?" the boy called to her from across the creek. He was kneeling by the water and poking a stick at something.

Wallace? He must have meant the dog. "I don't know him, actually. He's just been following me. And now I guess I'm following him."

"He's a pretty nice dog," the boy said. "I was afraid I'd be allergic to him, but I'm not. I'm allergic to a lot of other things, though."

"My brother's allergic." Abby set the cooler on the ground next to a large rock. She felt like she was in a safe place now and could take a minute to rest. "But we got the kind of dog that allergic people can live with."

"A bichon frise?"

"No, a cockapoo. He's really nice."

The boy nodded. "My dad says hypoallergenic dogs cost, like, seven hundred dollars."

"Yeah," Abby agreed. "They're expensive."

The boy stood up and wiped his hands on his jeans. "Do you come to this creek a lot?"

"This is the first time. I didn't even know it was here," Abby admitted.

"I come here all the time," the boy told her. "But I'm not allowed to cross over. It's beyond the safe perimeters. I'll get in a lot of trouble if I even think about it."

The boy's name, it turned out, was Anders, and he was older than he looked. Abby would have guessed seven, but it turned out he was almost nine. They stood across from each other for a few minutes while Anders told her some things about himself: He was being homeschooled by his grandmother, he liked the *Star Wars* movies and books, but he didn't like any *Clone Wars* stuff.

Abby waited for Anders to pause, but he just kept going. He was like Gabe talking at the breakfast table about a hockey game he'd seen on TV the night before, cramming in every single fact there was to report.

He was just starting to tell her about some science project he was doing, which involved separating groups of vertebrate animals into their different classes, when Wallace began to bark behind them. Something—or someone—was barreling down the path through the woods to the creek.

They were chasing her? They were really out to get her? Abby panicked. "Someone's after me!" she cried across the creek to Anders.

Anders waved both of his arms in wild circles. "Get over on this side! The water's hardly deep at all here—you can get across and run away!"

Abby didn't even know if it was Kristen and Georgia racing down the wooded path. It could have been some neighborhood kids. But Wallace howled and she thought maybe he knew something, so she splashed into the creek and crossed to the other side.

"Where can I go now?" she demanded after she'd scrambled up the bank.

Anders grabbed her arm. "Up the hill—come on!"

Together they ran away from the creek, through a jumble of brambles and bushes, up a craggy hill that seemed to go on forever, and finally they got to the top. Beyond the tree line was an open field.

When they reached the field, Abby flopped down on her back, trying to catch her breath. Could a person's lungs explode? She was pretty sure *her* lungs were about to explode. While she waited for that to happen, she wondered why some people could run for miles and not even breathe hard, and she couldn't go twenty yards without feeling like the air was being sucked from her throat with a vacuum cleaner. Even Claudia, who was terrible at most sports, could run without collapsing at the finish line. But not tubby Abby.

Anders sat down beside her. "Are you okay?"

"I guess," Abby told him, not 100 percent convinced. She sat up and examined her arms for scratches. "Except now I have to figure out how to get back home without getting caught."

"Who's trying to catch you? Are you in trouble with the police?"

"I'm in trouble with two very mean girls. That's much worse than the police, believe me."

Anders seemed to think about that for a minute. "So, what can they do to you? The girls, I mean."

"Well, they can—" Abby paused. How could she explain to an almost nine-year-old boy the terrible things girls did? The secret, down-low, parents-never-figure-it-out, terrible things that girls did to you if you were too fat or too skinny or had pimples or wore the wrong kind of jeans.

"They can kill you," she said after a moment. "Only, other people don't know that you're dead. Only you know, on the inside."

Anders stayed quiet for a long time after that. And then all he said was, "Yeah."

Wallace howled in the distance. When Abby looked up, she saw him across the field. "How did he get over there? Wasn't he just back at the creek a minute ago?"

"Wallace has powers," Anders told her. He stood up and held out his hand, and Abby grabbed it.

"I guess we better follow him, then," she said, scrambling to her feet. They took off running through the weeds and the clover, and though she still thought her lungs might explode, she didn't want to stop.

Chapter Ten

abby kept running, her chest on fire, and she was wondering when it was going to be time to stop running when she looked up and saw a farm.

A farm! What on earth was a farm doing in her neighborhood? Okay, looking around her, she had to admit that maybe she wasn't in her neighborhood anymore, but she wasn't that far away from it. So where did this farm come from, with its big red barn and whitewashed outbuildings, a split-rail fence enclosing a pasture? Abby sniffed the air. All around her were farm smells—

freshly mown grass, manure, and animals.

"There's horses in there," Anders told her, pointing toward the barn. They'd slowed to a walk by now. "Eight of 'em."

"You live here?" Abby asked.

"Well, I only sort of live here. Me and my dad are staying here with my grandmother until everything gets figured out."

Abby wanted to ask what needed figuring out, but she could tell by the way Anders was looking at the ground instead of at her that he didn't want to say anything else about it.

The house was on the other side of the field, close to the road, tucked in beneath a stand of oak trees. The wooden steps creaked as they walked up to the front door, which opened before they'd even made it to the porch. An old woman poked her head out.

"No more magazines, thanks," she said. "I've got all the magazines I need."

She started to close the door again, and Anders called out, "Grandma, it's me. And this is my friend Abby. She needs a ride home."

"Well, what are you hiding over there for?"

Anders's grandmother asked him, squinting in his general direction.

"Grandma, I'm right here," Anders protested. "You forgot to put on your glasses."

Anders's grandmother harrumphed. Then she turned to Abby. "We'll have to take the truck," she said. "Anders's dad took the Impala to pick up some things at Walmart."

She leaned forward, as if to get a better look at Abby. "You can call me Mrs. Benton, if you want to call me something. You thirsty? You look wrung out. Well, I've got orange juice. Let's get you something to drink before you collapse."

Abby stood there blinking, still trying to process what was happening. She was on a farm and someone was talking to her very rapidly about orange juice. Were Kristen and Georgia still looking for her? Well, they'd never find her now, would they?

Abby followed Anders and Mrs. Benton into the house. The blinds in the front room were closed, but there was enough light for Abby to see papers scattered everywhere and walls with pieces of torn-out notebook paper and maps and charts taped to them. She desperately wanted to read what was written on those pieces of paper, but she thought that she might be violating somebody's privacy if she did.

The kitchen was brighter. A picture window looked out over the field they'd just walked across, and now Abby could see the other side of the barn and a corral. Loose-leaf paper was stacked in messy piles on a round table in the corner of the room, and a huge encyclopedia was opened to a page on—Abby walked over to get a better look—foxes. Foxes!

"Are foxes part of your science project?" she asked Anders. "Because I saw a fox across from my house a couple days ago."

Anders's eyes widened. "A red fox?"

"I think so," Abby said. "Not bright red or anything. More rusty than red."

Anders looked at his grandmother and raised his eyebrows. "Did you hear that, Grandma?"

Mrs. Benton was pouring juice into two striped glasses. "I heard. That's good news. Anders's dad, Matt, is always talking about how much he'd like to see a fox. There used be lots of them around here, but the suburbs drove them out."

She handed Abby a glass. "I guess we ought to sit on the porch. Matt'll have a fit if we spill juice on his notes. We've been eating dinner on the couch for the last two months."

When they reached the porch, Mrs. Benton nodded toward two rocking chairs. "Sit down, you two. But no slouching."

Anders turned to Abby. "Grandma teaches horseback riding. You should probably try to remember to sit up straight and suck in your stomach around her."

"All the girls slouch these days! They've got no abdominal muscles, no core strength," Mrs. Benton complained, patting her belly. "Abdominals are the key to everything. Of course, I've spent half my life on horseback, so I've known that for ages. Ride tall in the saddle, that's my motto. Suck in your gut. That's my other motto."

Mrs. Benton settled onto the porch swing and turned to Abby, who had taken a seat in a rocking chair and was now trying to sit up as straight as possible. "You ride?"

Abby reddened and shook her head. Last

spring, after Claudia moved and Abby was trying to get in good with Kristen and Georgia, she'd claimed to be an expert on horses. She'd said she'd grown up riding horses on her grandmother's farm. She knew better than to lie to Mrs. Benton, though. She had the feeling that Mrs. Benton would throw her on the back of a horse just to make sure Abby was telling the truth.

"You should consider it," Mrs. Benton said. "In fact, why don't you come over Tuesday and eyeball my afternoon class? I need more students. I've got my Saturday morning class, and Thursdays are close to booked up, but that's not enough."

You couldn't pay Abby to get on top of a horse. She'd break her neck in a minute! Still, to be polite, she said, "I'll talk to my mom about it."

"Good, good. She'll be all for it, I'm sure," Mrs. Benton replied. "So, tell me about your fox. You say it was a red fox?"

Abby nodded. "Its fur was red. Well, like I said, brownish-red. It was little. And it didn't seem to be scared of me." Abby decided not to say anything about the fox biting her.

"Be interesting to know exactly what kind of fox it was. There's more than one species in these parts, if you go out into the countryside." Mrs. Benton leaned forward and peered at Abby. "You know much about the Lewis and Clark expedition? Ever study it in school?"

Where did that question come from? Was Mrs. Benton always this random? "I saw a special on PBS once," Abby offered. "My mom teaches history, so we watch a lot of PBS specials."

She could tell from Mrs. Benton's expression that she wanted more—that she was going to be disappointed if Abby couldn't come up with an interesting Lewis and Clark fact on the spot. "I remember that they had a dog," she offered lamely after a moment. "It was pretty furry."

Mrs. Benton nodded. "Seaman. Interesting character. We're doing a kind of Lewis and Clark study around here right now, and to be perfectly honest, we could use a little help."

"It's a family project," Anders put in. "Me, my dad, and Grandma." He turned to his grandmother. "Did I tell you what I read? They sent a prairie dog to President Jefferson in a box. Alive. And it made it there alive too."

"Did you tell Matt?" Mrs. Benton asked. "He'd want to know that."

"I'm going to tell him the nanosecond he gets home."

Mrs. Benton pushed herself up from the rocking chair with a groan. "I'll go find my keys and my glasses. Finish up your juice. I'm sorry my son's not here. It's good for him to meet new people. Maybe you could come back sometime. Help out with the project a little, if you've got a mind to."

"Okay," Abby said, feeling unsure. "Maybe."

"You could come back tomorrow," Anders said eagerly, like he couldn't think of anything more wonderful than another visit from Abby. "I'll show you the horses."

Abby only nodded. She liked Anders, and she wouldn't mind knowing what was written on all those pages tacked to the wall in the front room. But she could tell there was more going on here than you could figure out by just looking around. Something a little bit strange. Maybe more than a little bit. Why did Anders's father need to meet new people? Why did he want to see a fox so badly? He was a grown-up! What was so important about a prairie dog in a box? Why the pieces of paper everywhere? Why would you ask a total stranger to help you with a family project?

She felt a nudge against her leg and looked down to see Wallace. He looked up at her. There was a peculiar expression in his eyes. It was almost apologetic, but also firm. Abby leaned down and patted him on the head, and an electric buzz pulsed up through her fingertips. She remembered how he'd led her to the creek. Led her to Anders. Maybe it hadn't been an accident.

Maybe she was supposed to be here.

Chapter Eleven

when abby got home, her mother was in the kitchen making pizza. They always had homemade pizza on Saturday night, but Abby had mixed feelings about it. Because she loved pizza, she wanted to eat slice after slice until she was too full to eat one more bite, but what stunk was that she knew her parents would be watching her. Her mother's eyebrows would rise a little higher with each piece Abby ate, and her dad would make comments like, "Save some for the rest of us, Ab," which were supposed to sound like jokes. But Abby knew he wasn't joking.

"I'm going to make two sausage and one cheese," her mom announced when Abby walked into the kitchen. "But the sausage is for the boys and Dad, okay? You and I can share the cheese pizza."

"But I like sausage," Abby complained. "Why can't I eat sausage pizza?"

"Abby," her mom said, sounding as though Abby were being unreasonable. "Come on, sweetie, you don't need sausage. It's so fatty."

Abby didn't care if she didn't need sausage. She wanted sausage. Why should John and Gabe get to have sausage just because they were skinny? Fatty foods were bad for everybody, weren't they? If her brothers could eat foods that were bad for them, she should be able to, too.

"Fix the salad, would you, sweetie?" Her mom pointed to a bag of lettuce on the island in the middle of the kitchen. "And grate the carrots, don't chop them. Grated is nicer."

Abby opened the fridge and pulled out the carrots and a green pepper. She eyed the shelf with the salad dressing. Blue cheese, Thousand Island, and fat-free ranch. The fat-free ranch was for her. It tasted like garlicky glue with artificial sweetener stirred in. She wondered if she could sneak some Thousand Island on her salad when no one was looking.

By the time the pizza was on the table, Abby was starving. Her father was the official pizza cutter and server, and when it was Abby's turn, he put a single slice of cheese pizza on her plate. "Maybe that'll do ya, Ab, what do you think?"

Abby thought that one piece of cheese pizza would not do her, but she didn't say so. She took the plate from her dad and set it down in front of her. At least it wasn't a tiny piece, she consoled herself. At least it had some crust on it.

"What are you trying to do, starve her?" John asked, and Abby smiled at him for sticking up for her, even though she wished he wouldn't make a big deal out of it. She didn't want the dinner table discussion to be about her eating.

"You just worry about what's on your plate, John-Boy," Abby's dad said. "I'll worry about Abby."

Abby concentrated on tearing her paper napkin into tiny pieces on her lap. She wanted to yell, *Quit making a big deal about how much I eat! Just let me have some pizza!* But she didn't have the kind of dad you could yell at. You could maybe joke with him a little bit, but never yell.

"Oh, let's talk about something more interesting, why don't we," Abby's mom said in her peacemaker's voice. "Gabe, have you decided what you're going to wear for Colonial Day next week?"

Gabe had a mouthful of pizza, but that didn't stop him from answering. "You know what would be cool? A musket. Like, if I wore a sort of army uniform from back then and carried a musket."

"You're kidding, right?" John asked. "They're not going to let you bring a gun to school. Even a fake one."

"What if I made it out of a stick or something? So no one would think it was real?"

"No way," John insisted. "No weapons, period. They'll expel you."

Abby's mom's eyes widened. "From second grade? For a stick?"

"Yeah, Mom, for a stick. They'll expel you for

anything. Like if you brought some aspirin in your backpack and your teacher found it? Automatic expulsion."

Abby's mom shook her head. "I don't want Gabe bringing a stick to school, but that seems so extreme to me."

"I don't make the rules," John said, reaching for another slice of sausage pizza.

Abby was taking tiny bites of her pizza, trying to eat it as slowly as possible. She had one eye on the bottle of Thousand Island. It was within her reach, but could she grab it without anyone noticing? No, she shouldn't grab. Grabbing would definitely get her noticed. But maybe she could reach over casually, like it was no big deal. That was it—she would ask Gabe a question, get him talking, and while everyone was listening to him, she'd just sort of quietly move the Thousand Island closer to her. And then she'd really nonchalantly put a little bit on her salad—

"Hey, Ab," her dad said, interrupting her strategizing. "Did you get any exercise today?"

Abby sucked in her stomach, thinking of Mrs. Benton. "I took a walk," she said. "It was nice."

"Walking is good," her dad said, but Abby could tell he didn't mean it. "How about jogging? Great for your heart, and it really burns the calories."

Abby's mom shook her head. "Oh, let's not talk about calories at the dinner table," she said lightly. "That's no fun."

"Well, look at her, Susan. Someone should talk to her about calories." Her dad turned back to Abby. "Calories in, calories out. That's the formula, Ab. You have to burn more calories than you take in. That's all there is to it."

Abby looked at her pizza. One-third of her slice was left. She knew it was getting cold and she should hurry up and eat it since she didn't like cold pizza, but suddenly there was a lump in her throat and she thought she might not be able to swallow right now.

"Hey, Dad, did you lift weights when you were in high school?" John asked. "Because Coach was saying he didn't think we should really get into lifting until sophomore year. It might do some damage if we start earlier."

Good old John, always changing the subject.

When dinner was over, Abby helped her mom clear the table. She tried to remember to keep her gut sucked in. She liked how it made her feel taller. She wondered if holding in your stomach burned extra calories. And did you have to hold it in all the time? She'd have to ask Mrs. Benton if you were allowed to let your stomach out every once in a while.

"Hey, Mom," Abby said, dumping out left-over salad into the trash. "Do you have any books on Lewis and Clark?"

"I'm sure I do, down in the basement." Her mom glanced over at Abby from the sink. "Do you need them for school?"

"For a project," Abby told her. "I thought I might get started tonight."

Drying her hands on a dish towel, Abby's mom said, "I'll go see what I have." She sounded excited. "I think I have that book that won all the prizes. It's wonderful."

Abby's mom disappeared down the basement stairs. Abby looked around. She was alone. Her dad and brothers were in the family room watching a college football game on TV. There were three pieces of sausage pizza on the platter on top of the stove. Abby stepped softly over to the paper towels and pulled off two sheets. Quietly, she crept to the stove and wrapped two of the pieces in the paper towels. They were still warm. She could smell the sausage.

The trick would be sneaking past the family room without her dad seeing she had something in her hand. Because if he noticed her carrying something wrapped in paper towels as she headed toward the stairs, something that might be food, he would definitely want to know what it was.

Her left-hand side would be toward the family room, so she should carry the pizza in her right hand. Could she put it in a book? No, she'd get pizza grease all over the pages. Abby looked around the kitchen. The newspaper. She could put the paper-towel-wrapped pizza in the news-paper, and then if anyone asked, she could say she was taking the paper to cut out articles for a current events assignment.

Brilliant.

Abby ate the pizza sitting at her desk. She

took bite after humongous bite, the sausage and cheese and crust filling up her mouth and making her whole body hum. Why did food taste so good? Abby wondered about this a lot. Because if food didn't taste so good, she wouldn't have a problem. She would get this lovely, filled-up feeling from something else. There were books that almost made her feel filled up the way pizza did, usually books she wasn't supposed to read, celebrity biographies her mother called "trashy," and books she was officially too old to read, like Junie B. Jones. Candy books.

She was halfway through the second piece when her mom knocked on her door. "Abby, I found it! *Undaunted Courage*—that's the title. May I come in?"

Abby scrambled to wrap the remaining pizza in the newspaper and throw it into her trash can. She sniffed the air around her desk. Could you still smell sausage?

"Come in," she called, trying to sound innocent. "I'm just doing some homework."

"You are so good to do homework on Saturday night," her mother said as she walked into the room. "I always used to wait until the last minute, and it made Sundays so depressing."

She stopped, cocked her head to the side. "It smells funny in here. What is that?"

"I know, it's weird!" Abby exclaimed, jumping to her feet. "My shirt totally smells like pizza! Isn't that weird?"

"It's the sausage," her mom said, nodding her head in agreement. "Whenever I cook sausage for the pizza, the house smells like sausage for the rest of the night. Well, anyway, here's the book."

She handed it to Abby, who nearly dropped it. "Sort of heavy," Abby said, putting the book down on her desk. "Thanks, though. I thought I'd see if I could find some interesting facts."

To Abby's dismay, her mother sat down on her bed. If she hung out in Abby's room much longer, she might sniff out the pizza wrapped up in newspaper. "Oh, the Lewis and Clark story is fascinating. Thomas Jefferson sent them out West. He was a genius, Jefferson. Remember that trip we took to Monticello?"

"It was fun," Abby said, though mostly what

she remembered was how obsessed the tour guide was with the beds, which where built into the walls of the rooms. "We should go back sometime."

Abby's mom smiled. "We should. It's only a few hours away. And now that Gabe's class is studying colonial America . . . That reminds me! Costume! I think there might be something in the back of John's closet from a play he did—"

With that, Abby's mom was up and out of her room. Abby staggered to her bed and plopped down. Whew! That was close! She could just imagine what she'd have to go through if her mom had found the pizza. A lecture from her dad about being a big fat pig, that was for sure. And then maybe they'd put her back on an official diet instead of just bugging her about what she ate, and there'd be low-fat yogurt at every meal. And packaged turkey slices. Abby hated packaged turkey slices.

She got up and dug the half piece of pizza out of her trash can. It was cold and the fat was starting to congeal on the sausage. But the crust? The crust still looked good. Abby tore it off and started to chew. She reached under her bed and pulled out *Junie B. Jones Is Not a Crook*. She thought about crying, but she decided to keep chewing instead.

Chapter Twelve

that night, when the fox woke
up from yet another dream of bombs exploding,
she made her way through the yards, across the
street, and down to the creek. No fish, unless you
counted the swarms of tiny minnows, which the
fox did not. Minnows! When once she had dined
on red-and-orange cutthroat trout.

She'd been in the long-ago story of the grand
expedition, on a narrow boat floating westward on
the lazy river. Everything had seemed so new,
even the sky. The wind like God laughing softly in
the next room. She'd folded herself into a bundle

behind the boxes of supplies and piles of blankets, and when she got hungry, she reached a paw over the side and grabbed a fish from the water.

Tall tale! Crow had cawed when she'd told him about it later. *Tall tale!*

But birds fished the river all the time. Why not a fox, so much smarter than a bird in every way? *Yes, all I had to do was reach a paw out,* the fox had insisted to Crow, who'd flown away nattering like a cranky old man.

The old story soothed the fox, even with the echoes of Crow's disbelieving cries ringing in her ears. Really, she had to do something about these nightmares. Who'd ever heard of a fox having nightmares? Preposterous! What if that silly raccoon found out, the one that had set up shop by the trash bins next door to the fox's field? The fox could hear its snitty laughter. Raccoons always sounded like they were choking when they laughed. Disgusting.

When she reached the creek, the water was cool, and it calmed her as she drank from it. When she was done, she lifted her nose to a familiar scent and realized she could smell the girl she now knew was named Abby. She looked around and saw a small cooler a few feet away from where she stood. Too small for Abby to be inside. She must have touched it, carried it, left it here on the way to somewhere else.

"Abby," the girls had called out when they came into the fox's field that afternoon. "Oh, Abby," in sickly sweet voices, like the voice a raccoon might use to woo its poor, pitiful excuse for a mate. The fox didn't think the girls—sallow-faced, scrawny things—should be there in the field, but she decided to give them one chance to prove her wrong.

They screamed when they saw her. Of course. One even scrambled wildly for something to throw, and so the fox had pulled back her lips to reveal her sharp incisors, which—of course— sent the girls running.

Abby. The girl's name was Abby, and these two scrawny raccoon girls were after her. The fox had followed them to the edge of the field, watched them hop onto their bikes, calling to each other, "Don't worry, we'll find her, and then she'll be sorry!"

Well. Best not to think of that. Better to think of the long boat, and the grasses that lined the river, redolent of fish and mud. Think of the young men, who built fires at night when they stopped to camp and sat in a circle around them, singing. One man played fiddle, and the others called out the songs they wanted to hear, "Soldier's Joy," "Bonaparte's Retreat." And one man—a very young man—kept getting lost. But he was found, again and again, and each time he returned, the men sang louder and laughed harder, the world around them new and theirs for the taking.

Chapter Thirteen

abby hadn't planned on going back to Anders's house on Sunday. Oh, she'd go sometime, she'd thought, but not the next day. It seemed too soon, almost like if she showed up at the Bentons' on Sunday afternoon, she was agreeing to help them with their Lewis and Clark project, and she didn't know if she wanted to help them. She didn't even *know* them.

So, on Sunday morning, she lay in bed and started reading *Undaunted Courage*, about the Lewis and Clark expedition. It wasn't the sort of book she usually read, with its ten million facts and official-sounding sentences, but she found if she skipped around, there were good parts hidden behind the dates and weights and treaties, parts that were more like a story and less like homework. She wished there were more girls in the book, though she knew if she kept reading, Sacagawea would show up sooner or later.

She was trying to decide whether to keep slogging through or get dressed and see if her mom would make her French toast for breakfast ("It's just bread and eggs, Mom," she would argue, "bread and eggs have hardly any calories"), when she came across the story of George Shannon. What first got her interest was the fact that George Shannon was only seventeen. There was a famous actor Abby liked who was seventeen, and she imagined George Shannon with the actor's high cheekbones and scruffy brown hair and the way he had of looking at people through half-closed eyes. Picturing George Shannon this way made Abby want to keep reading, which was how she learned the amazing fact that George Shannon had gotten lost two times on the Lewis and Clark expedition—once for sixteen days without food or water—and that each time he'd found his way back on his own.

Now that, Abby thought when she finished reading about George Shannon, *is a good story.*

So after breakfast she put on her shoes and her jacket and headed across the street to her field, and after she'd looked to see if any new birds were around, she climbed over the fence and walked down to the creek, where Wallace was waiting for her.

What surprised her about this was that she wasn't surprised at all.

Anders was sitting on the front porch when she came around to the front of the Bentons' house. "My dad's here!" Anders greeted her, standing. "I told him all about you. He's really excited to meet you!"

"How did you know I was coming?" Abby asked.

Anders shrugged. "I just knew you would."

"Hey, Matt," Anders called as he led Abby into the house. "Abby's here!"

Anders's father was sitting at the round table in the kitchen, writing on a piece of loose-leaf notebook paper. He looked up when they entered the room, and Abby took a step back, startled by his face, how handsome it was, and how he seemed frightened. He had dark circles under his eyes and a couple of days' worth of stubble on his cheeks. His hair and eyes were black as crows' wings.

"This is Abby," Anders explained to him. "She's the girl we told you about."

Relief, then a smile bloomed on the man's face. "Wallace brought you."

"I guess you could say that," Abby agreed, and then wondered if that sounded stupid. Suddenly she felt fumbly and tongue-tied. Anders's dad was so handsome! "He led me down to the creek yesterday, and that's where I met Anders."

"On this side of the creek," Anders put in. "Don't worry. I didn't cross it."

"Wallace is my dog," Anders's father told Abby. "Or he was. Now he's more Mom's than mine. I got him right after high school, taught him how to track. He knows the woods around here better than anybody."

And then suddenly, without warning, he

pounded a fist on the table and said in a strangled voice, "I have to write, I have to write."

Anders tapped Abby on the arm. "Why don't we go find Grandma? Matt, you call me if you need me."

"Your dad is really good-looking," Abby whispered as they went through the hallway to the front room. "It's sort of amazing."

"He used to look a lot better," Anders informed her. "Before he went to Iraq. Iraq kind of took a lot out of him."

Mrs. Benton was sitting on the porch swing, reading a newsletter called *Riding Instructor*. "This thing is written by idiots," she declared in way of a greeting. "It's all about dressage and tail braiding. Complete waste of time." She slapped the newsletter to the floor, then looked at Abby. "You survived to live another day, I see. Anders told me about your troubles. Girls can be rough, but you'll be fine."

"I'm okay for now," Abby assured her, sitting down in a rocker. "I'm good." She studied Mrs. Benton's face, looking for any resemblance to her

99

son. They both had the same dark brown eyes, the same little dimple in their chins, but Mrs. Benton's features were sharper than Matt's, her nose pointier, her lips thinner. She had deep worry lines etched into her forehead, which Abby found interesting—Mrs. Benton didn't strike her as the worrying type. She sounded so sure of herself all the time, like she could take care of any problem that came her way. But then Abby thought about Matt, the way he'd looked so afraid when she'd walked in the kitchen, and she guessed there might be some problems that Mrs. Benton couldn't do anything about.

"Grandma, did you remind Matt to take his pills?" Anders asked his grandmother, taking a seat next to her on the swing. "'Cause he's acting a little aggravated in there."

Mrs. Benton looked pained. "I told him to take them, but I can't force them down his throat."

"He's got to take the pills, Grandma! Just give them to him like he was a kid. Put them in a spoonful of peanut butter." Anders shook his head. "You act like he's going to take care of himself, but he won't."

He turned to Abby. "My dad has got some problems, the main one being that he doesn't really want to live anymore."

Anders's grandmother winced and then made a strange sound from deep in her throat, the sort of sound Abby woke herself up with when she was having a nightmare.

"Our job is to make sure he doesn't do anything stupid," Anders went on, shooting his grandmother a look. "Our job is to keep him alive."

Abby rocked back and forth for a moment without saying anything, without having any idea of what to say. Finally she asked, hoping it was okay to ask, "Where's your mom?"

"Virginia. Springfield," Anders said without a trace of expression in his voice. "She lives there with her sister."

"Anders's mom and dad aren't together anymore," Mrs. Benton informed Abby. "It's complicated."

"Not really." Anders wriggled in his seat, clearly agitated. "My dad did two tours of duty in Iraq, and me and my mom stayed in Virginia, and when my dad came home the last time, my mom decided she didn't want to be married to him anymore because the war had changed him so much."

"Well," Mrs. Benton said, and Abby could tell she was trying to be diplomatic. "Well. Yes. But she's young, and she didn't plan on"—she waved her hand around in a vague sort of way—"this situation, I guess is one way you could put it."

"You're supposed to stay married for better or worse," Anders said. "That's the promise."

Her grandmother nodded, stared blankly ahead. "Yes, I suppose it is."

"Did you know that Lewis and Clark discovered over a hundred twenty mammal specimens?" Abby said after the quiet had been stretched thin and she was starting to feel awkward, like she had stumbled into a private family conversation she really shouldn't be listening to. "I've been sort of reading this book my mom gave me."

Mrs. Benton nodded toward the door. "That's what he's in there writing about. All the zoological specimens they found along the way. He's making a list, describing everything. His poem, he calls it. That's what's all over the walls—his notes, the charts he's drawn up. He got interested after I told him about a book I was reading about the expedition."

"'It was an undiscovered world,' he keeps saying," Anders reported. "'Everything was new.'"

"He says if he finishes the poem, then maybe he'll be okay, so we're all working on it together." Mrs. Benton pushed herself up out of the swing with a groan. "At least it gives him something to focus on. I'm going to get him to take his pills."

The screen door slammed behind her. Anders looked at Abby and shook his head. "I keep thinking about that prairie dog. I still can't believe he made it east alive," he said. And then he added, "It almost gives you hope."

When Mrs. Benton came back, she handed Abby a piece of paper. "This is a partial list of animals we still need to do research on. Why don't you take it with you? Look a few things up, if you've got the time."

"You want me to help?" she asked Mrs. Benton after she'd read the list. "With the research? But you don't even know if I'm good at stuff like that."

"Oh, I can tell. You went home last night and started reading, didn't you? You've got curiosity, and you know how to get your hands on a book. And"—Mrs. Benton paused and looked Abby straight in the eye—"you came back."

"I told you she would," Anders said. "I knew it."

"The fact is, we need you," Mrs. Benton continued. She nodded toward Anders. "Right now, there's only two of us. And Matt, of course, but he has his good days and his bad days and can't always concentrate."

"Couldn't a doctor help him?" Abby asked. "I mean, help him with his feelings?"

"A doctor *is* helping him," Mrs. Benton said. "And we're trying to get him a place at the Veterans Administration hospital, but with all the budget cuts, they're short on space."

"It would be great if you could help," Anders said. "I mean, anything you could do. It would be great."

So Abby agreed.

On Tuesday, Anoop gave Abby one of his *dosas* for lunch and Jafar gave her half of a chicken salad sandwich. Her lunch had disappeared, and though she was sure Kristen was responsible, Abby couldn't figure out how she'd done it. She remembered putting her lunch bag in her locker when she'd gotten to school that morning, and she didn't think anyone else knew her combination.

"Maybe you gave your combination to a friend, but forgot?" Jafar suggested.

"But even if that were so," Anoop countered, "why would her friend take her lunch?"

Jafar thought for a moment. "She was hungry. Or maybe she needed to take a pill. When I take my allergy medicine, I always have to eat something, or else I get dizzy."

"Then why didn't she eat her own lunch?" Anoop asked.

"Maybe her locker is on the other side of the building."

"Well, if this is the case, Abby's friend should have come forward and offered to buy Abby another lunch. I don't think her friend is much of a friend."

While Anoop and Jafar argued across the table from her, Abby observed them, as if she were going to draw their pictures next to the birds in her notebook. Anoop was neat. He parted his dark hair on the side, so you could see the thin, pale line of his scalp. His white shirt was buttoned at the collar, and he had folded his sleeves twice so that they rested mid-forearm. His fingernails were very clean, his posture impressively straight. If he were a bird, he would be a shiny black raven.

Jafar reminded Abby of her little brother, Gabe. His hair was shaggy, his smile lopsided and friendly, and his Atlanta Braves T-shirt had food stains on it. When she showed up at lunch on Friday, he'd exclaimed, "Excellent! Finally someone who will listen to my jokes without making old-lady faces."

Jafar, she was pretty sure, would be a humming-bird, filled with happiness.

She was amazed how easy it was to sit with them. For one thing, she wasn't always trying to figure out the right thing to say. With girls, you had to be careful; if you said something wrong, it could set off a chain reaction that would leave you sitting by yourself while everyone else hung out by the monkey bars and laughed louder than normal, just so you'd be sure to hear how much fun they were having without you. But while Anoop was irritable, he wasn't mean, and Jafar reminded her of a puppy who was just happy to be with people.

Is this how it is with boys? Abby wondered as she bit into her *dosa*. *You just talk about stuff?*

She peered across the cafeteria, wondering if there were girls she could be friends with as easily as she'd become friends with Anoop and Jafar. After all, Claudia had been an amazing friend, nothing at all like Kristen or Georgia.

She could still remember the day after Claudia moved, in the very middle of fifth grade. Abby had gotten on the school bus and hadn't had a single, solitary person to sit with. She'd spent the bumpy ride to school thinking about how lonely she was going to be for the rest of her life without Claudia. No friends. No one to write notes to or have sleepovers with. No one to build shoe-box apartments with.

As Abby looked around the cafeteria, her eye fell on Marlys Barry, who was sitting by herself, writing in a spiral notebook. She remembered with a twinge how Marlys—poor Marlys with the name no one could say, who had to explain at the beginning of every school year that it was pronounced Mar-liss, and still the teachers forgot—had invited her to eat lunch with her a few days after Claudia had moved, and Abby was going to, only Kristen had overheard their conversation and took Abby aside.

"Listen, you really don't want to eat lunch with her," Kristen had whispered, holding tight to Abby's arm, squeezing it a little bit. "You should eat at my table. And why don't you sit with me on the bus home?"

Abby had found Kristen's offer impossible to refuse. Kristen lived in her neighborhood, but they'd never been friends, not really. Kristen had had too many sharp edges for Abby to feel comfortable around her. She was the sort of girl who was always leaning over and whispering in somebody's ear while giving someone else the evil eye. In their neighborhood, she'd been powerful and best avoided, though at school she wasn't that important.

But Abby had been flattered that Kristen seemed to be looking out for her. So she told Marlys she'd forgotten she'd promised to eat lunch with Kristen, but maybe they could eat lunch together another time. Marlys had said sure, fine, but she'd never gone out of her way again to be friendly.

Of course, now Abby knew she'd picked the wrong person to have lunch with. What if she'd eaten with Marlys that day? Would they have liked each other? Abby saw Marlys hanging out in the computer lab a lot—maybe she was some sort of computer geek, like John's friend Travis, who was obsessed with creating role-playing games and making animated videos. Abby didn't think she'd want someone who spent all her time on the computer for a best friend. That would get boring fast.

Still, Marlys was probably great at doing computer research, Abby thought, reaching over and taking a handful of grapes from Jafar's lunch box. Abby was terrible at doing research on the computer—there was always too much information to choose from when she was writing a report. How was she supposed to know what was important and what wasn't? She hated doing research, period. She liked stories better than facts, and research was all about facts.

So why, oh why, had she told Mrs. Benton she would help with the Benton family's project? Abby munched irritably on a grape and tried to figure out how she'd gotten into this mess, wondering if there was any way out.

There were fifteen minutes left in the lunch period, and Abby supposed she'd better get started with her research, as much as she really didn't want to. When she got to the computer lab, she noticed that Marlys was already there. Much to her surprise, when Marlys saw Abby in the doorway, she waved her over to her desk. "Georgia took your lunch, in case you're interested," Marlys said in a low voice. "I heard her talking about it in art. She called your mom last night and got your locker combination. She told your mom that she was planning a surprise for you. She threw your lunch box away in the girls' room near the front office."

Abby sat down at the desk across the aisle from Marlys. Why did Georgia hate her so much? Because she'd stopped eating lunch with the medium girls? You'd think Georgia would be glad she was gone. "I guess that shouldn't really surprise me," Abby said, dropping her backpack on the chair next to her.

"No, it probably shouldn't," Marlys agreed, and turned back to her screen.

Abby entered her password into the computer, then peeked at Marlys while she waited for the school's home page to come up. She never would have thought Marlys was the sort of person who eavesdropped on other people's conversations. For one thing, she didn't act like she was all that interested in other people. Thinking about it, Abby realized she only ever saw Marlys by herself, either tapping away on a computer here in the lab or else sitting in the cafeteria taking notes in a notebook—but about what? Was she writing down what people were saying? Was she a spy?

Abby nodded to herself. She bet Marlys was a great spy. Quiet people paid the best attention.

And great spies probably made great researchers. Oh, if only Abby had accepted Marlys's lunch invitation that day! Then maybe they'd be friends, and right now Marlys could be helping her figure out the best way to find information on the bushy-tailed woodrat.

Abby sighed. She typed "bushy-tailed woodrat" into the search engine box. 15,904 results popped up on her screen. *Great,* she thought, *just great.* She pushed her hand through her bangs and twisted some of the hair around her fingers. It was going to take her ten million years to get this done. She wasn't going to be any help to the Bentons at all.

Chapter Fourteen

riding the bus home that afternoon, Abby smoothed out the sheet of paper Mrs. Benton had given her on Sunday and started reading it again. *Bushy-tailed woodrat, mule deer, pronghorn, white-tailed jack-rabbit, Columbian ground squirrel . . .*

Leaning back in her seat, Abby tried to imagine what some of the animals might look like. What in the world could a pronghorn be? She pictured a deer with a plug on top of its head. But Lewis and Clark wouldn't have named something based on electrical appliances. They didn't even have electrical appliances in 1804. Hmm. Something else, then. A horse with antlers?

She thought of the horses she'd met on Sunday when Anders had taken her on a tour of the stables. There were eight in all, although only three belonged to the Bentons; the others were horses they stabled for other people. Two of the horses were jet-black, and another one was a beautiful golden brown, like the color of fall leaves. All the horses had whinnied at Anders and Abby as they'd walked through the stables, poking their noses over their stalls and snorting.

They had all been absolutely huge. How in the world could anybody sit on top of one of those things? It would be like riding on top of a school bus.

Abby told herself to just imagine them with prongs growing out of their heads, and giggled a little. She still hadn't decided whether to go watch Mrs. Benton's riding lesson at four o'clock. Even with the silly picture of prong-horned horses in her head, she couldn't help feel a little nervous thinking about the humongous animals in the Bentons' stable.

What if she went and Mrs. Benton tried to get her to ride one? She'd feel silly standing in front of the other students and saying no thanks, not today, maybe some other time. They'd probably look at her and think she was too fat to get on a horse anyway.

I could just go watch, Abby thought. *I wouldn't even have to get near the horses.*

She thought about the swishing sound the horses' tails made as they flicked flies off their haunches. Like a straw broom sweeping out a cabin. Like Snow White making the little house nice and neat before the seven dwarves got home from work. *Swish, swish.* It was one of the nicest sounds Abby had ever heard.

She could just watch. She could watch from some place Mrs. Benton couldn't see her.

There were six riders in the ring when Abby reached the Bentons' farm. They all wore hard black hats, and five of them had on cream-colored jodhpurs and high leather riding boots. The sixth one, who was riding the golden-brown horse Abby thought was so beautiful, had on jeans and sneakers.

"That's Louise," Anders informed Abby when he and Wallace came to stand beside her at the far side of the barn, where Abby felt she was at a safe distance from any suggestions that she get on a horse. "She's Grandma's best rider, but she can't afford a horse or any of the gear. So Grandma lets her muck the stalls for lessons. And she lets her ride Ruckus whenever she wants."

"That's really nice of your grandmother."

Anders shrugged. "It's a win-win for everybody."

Abby caught the laugh coming out of her throat before it had a chance to escape. Some of the things that Anders said cracked her up, but she could tell he wasn't like Gabe, who didn't mind being laughed at. Maybe Anders was trying to sound like a grown-up because he had to act like a grown-up when it came to his dad. That thought sobered Abby up.

"Do you ride?" she asked, wondering what it

would be like to live surrounded by horses. Maybe if you saw horses every day, the idea of riding one wouldn't be so frightening.

"No, not really. I mean I used to, when we visited in the summers. But now my dad—" Anders paused, like he was embarrassed to continue. "Well, my dad worries about me getting thrown, or trampled. It's stupid! I mean, I know how to ride a horse already, and I never got thrown off, not even when I was six! It makes Grandma really mad. She gets mad at my dad for worrying about everything. For being afraid of everything. He didn't used to be, but now a lot of things scare him. Like if you accidentally drop a book on the floor? My dad jumps sky-high."

"My mom's a nervous person too," Abby said. "Not like your dad or anything, but she's always worried about people being unhappy or mad at each other. She's always trying to smooth things over. She hates it when anybody yells. That makes her super nervous."

Anders nodded. "Matt doesn't like yelling either. But the funny thing is, he yells all the time. Mostly at night, in his dreams. But some-times during the day, too. Stuff just gets to him more than it does other people."

Abby glanced toward the house. She wondered where Matt was. Was it okay to leave him alone? She sort of wanted to see him—was he really as handsome as she remembered?—but at the same time she didn't. What if he came outside right now and started yelling at her and Anders? What if he had a gun? He'd been a soldier, so he might have a gun. Suddenly Abby shivered. What was she doing here? She might not even be safe.

Abby looked at Anders. They wouldn't let him live in the same house as Matt if Matt were dangerous, right?

"Suck in your gut!" Mrs. Benton yelled, and Abby sucked in her gut before she realized that Mrs. Benton was yelling at her students, not her.

"Come on," Anders said, tugging on Abby's arm. "I'll show you where we have our pick-your-own patches. There's a strawberry patch and blueberry bushes. In May, when the strawberries come in, we get about a hundred people a day. Oh, and I can show you the beehives, too. They're way on the other end of the farm, away from the horses."

Beehives? *Great*, Abby thought as she followed Anders around the side of the barn. *Something even scarier than horses.* "So you guys keep bees?"

"Yeah, Grandma set up these hives a few years ago, and now it's Matt's big project, raising honeybees and selling their honey. He used to have hives when he was growing up."

"Don't the bees make him nervous?" Abby asked. "Isn't he scared of them?"

"You'd think he would be," Anders agreed. "But bees don't bother him at all. Most animals don't, except for horses. He spends a lot of the day outside, if the weather's good. And when he's inside, he's writing stuff down about animals."

Matt was pruning blueberry bushes when Abby and Anders reached the other side of the farm. "Hey, guys!" he called when he saw them, waving his pruning shears in their direction. "You didn't happen to bring any water with you, did you?"

"Sorry!" Anders called out. "We're dry. We came over to look at the hives."

Matt laid down his shears. "Great idea. I'll come with you. I haven't checked on my guys since Friday."

They walked into a brushy area that reminded Abby of the field across from her house, the weeds shedding their seeds, the leaves on the bushes turning scarlet.

Anders pointed ahead. "The hives are just about fifty yards that way. We keep them back here so they can have a little privacy."

"And to protect them from the wind," Matt explained. "They need some space, but they need protection from the elements, too."

Abby studied Matt from the corner of her eye. He looked better today, like he'd gotten a good night's sleep since the last time she'd seen him. Still, being near him made her nervous. What if somebody stepped on a stick and it made a loud crack? Would Matt start screaming? Would he come after Abby like she was the enemy?

Matt caught her looking at him. "Okay, don't kill me," he said, grinning. "But what was your name again? Anders told me, but my short-term memory is on the fritz these days. It's the pills the doc makes me take."

"It's Ab—"

Abby started to say her name was Abby, but something stopped her. Maybe it was the tingling near the spot on her hand where the fox had bitten her.

"It's Abigail," she finished.

"It is?" Anders looked confused. "I thought you said—"

Abby nodded. "It's Abigail. My mom and dad call me Abby sometimes. Abby's like my childhood nickname."

Matt nodded. "My folks used to call me Mattie. Got to a point where it drove me nuts."

The hives didn't look like what Abby had expected. She'd imagined lumpy domes, like oversize wasps' nests, but instead Matt's beehives were more like file boxes piled one on top of another. As they got closer, Abby could hear the buzzing from inside the hives. She glanced anxiously at Matt. "Are you going to open the hives up?"

Matt laughed. "Not without a smoker and protective gear. Nah, I just wanted to hear 'em. This is a strange time of year for bees. Most of the flowers have stopped blooming, and their work's about done. But they're not quite down for winter. I like to check in with them every few days, just to make sure everything's cool."

The three of them stood at a distance from the hives and listened. "Bees have an amazing way of communicating with each other," Matt told Abby. "They dance. They dance to tell each other where the food is, and whether or not it's good food, how much there is. Who knows what they're in there telling each other right now?"

"You're not scared of them?" Abby asked, unable to believe that what Anders said was true, that bees didn't make Matt nervous at all.

Matt shook his head. "Bees are predictable. Every once in a while there's a swarm, but most of the time bees do what they're supposed to do, unlike, say, people or horses. You don't know what's going to spook a horse"—and here he looked at Anders—"or when it's going to happen."

Anders turned away, and Abby saw him roll his eyes. "*Some* horses spook," he told his dad when he'd turned around again. "Nervous horses spook. Grandma's horses do not spook."

"Snake shows up in the grass, a horse is going to spook," Matt argued. "I don't care how steady he is the rest of the time."

Matt had seemed cheerful and happy only a moment before, but now his expression darkened. Abby looked at Anders, who had his eyes closed, as though he were trying to steady himself.

Abby wished she could think of something to say that would get them back to the dancing bees. She wished standing so close to Matt didn't make her feel uneasy. Most of the adults Abby knew stayed the same all the time. Her mother was always worried, even when she tried to cover it up by acting extra cheerful, and her dad was always bossy in his joke-around way. But Matt seemed to change all the time. One second he was happy-go-lucky, and the next he looked like he might explode.

I think I need to go home, Abby practiced

saying in her head. Or, *Sorry, I just remembered I had homework to do!* Homework. That was it.

"I bet you're scared of horses too."

Matt stood in front of Abby. "I mean, you seem like a reasonable person to me. And reasonable people stay away from horses, am I right?"

There was an edge to Matt's voice. He was smiling, but his smile wasn't friendly. And although he was looking straight at her, he didn't seem to see her.

"They're pretty big, it's true." Abby took a few steps back. "But I like them. In theory, I like them a lot."

"But they scare you, don't they?" Matt pressed. He sounded like a lawyer on a TV show.

"Dad." Anders stepped between Matt and Abby. "Dad."

Matt shook his head, as though he were waking up from a nap. "What?"

"Dad," Anders repeated. "Leave Abby alone."

Matt's eyes and mouth suddenly sagged. "Oh, yeah. Man. Abigail, I'm sorry."

Abby stood very still. She thought she might cry, but she held it in. She shoved her hands into her pockets so no one would see them shake.

"We better go back now," Anders said. "Abby probably has to go home."

They started walking, Matt lagging a little behind, Anders urging him to keep up. Abby looked at the trees and bushes on either side of the path, looked up at the darkening sky. She wished Matt would move faster. She didn't want to have to walk back down through the woods to the creek in the dark.

She thought about George Shannon lost on the prairie and wondered what it was like for him at night, with the million stars above and coyotes howling in the distance. Scary, probably. And lonely. Did he know how to make a fire by rubbing two sticks together? Did he lean back against a rock and sing, trying to make it sound like there were a bunch of people there, not just one seventeen-year-old boy?

Abby slowed her pace to let Matt catch up. Reminded herself that George Shannon had found his way back. He didn't stay lost forever.

Chapter Fifteen

the fox's hackles unexpectedly shot up, and she felt them even before she saw them—the girls. The scrawny raccoon girls were back. She watched them from her field as they slunk around Abby's house, peering in the first-floor windows.

"I bet she's inside, but she's pretending like she's not home," she heard one of the girls say from the front porch. "She was on the bus."

"I still don't get what we're supposed to say," the other girl complained. "I bet Abby's made up a bunch of lies about us to tell her mom. They probably won't even invite us in."

"First we'll say we're coming by to tell them that we saw a fox in the neighborhood and my mom called animal control, but they haven't found it yet. And then we'll figure out some way to make Abby's mom ask us in."

The girls disappeared into the backyard, and the fox could hear their footsteps crunching through the woods. She knew that Abby wasn't inside the house. She'd come to the field after school and sat in her chair for a while, drawing pictures in a book. And then she'd set off for the creek. The fox had followed her for a while, but then she'd smelled purple berries—a fat, juicy smell that pulled her back into the field.

Really, being a vegetarian wasn't so bad, not when the berries were still sweet.

The fox nipped at a branch and caught a berry between her teeth. Animal control, eh? Did anyone think animal control had a chance against her? All she had to do was make a set of tracks going to the left, and another going off to the right, and the poor fools would be so confused, they wouldn't know which direction to head in. They'd walk around in circles for days, months, years.

No, animal control wasn't a problem, only a nuisance. But these girls. These raccoons in training. Or perhaps weasels? Because raccoons were clowns, but weasels were mean. Low-down. The fox never trafficked with them if she could help it.

The weasel girls were after Abby.

The fox began pacing in circles. Maybe there was something she could do. Something more than just watch.

The fox had always watched. She was known for standing to the side and letting the action unfold. Observing, always observing. She was not unaffected by what she saw (the children standing by the bedside, their mother covered with pox; the great ship sinking into the frigid waters; the line of men waiting for a cup of soup and a chunk of bread), but she didn't step forth. Didn't try to make things different from what they were.

Maybe it was time.

Maybe then the nightmares would stop.

Chapter Sixteen

the first thing Abby thought about when she woke up on Saturday was the migrating pronghorn, also known as the pronghorn antelope, even though it wasn't an antelope at all, but a species of artiodactyl mammal, which is to say, an even-toed ungulate. Pronghorns, Abby now knew, had wandered the face of the earth for more than two million years, if the fossil record was correct. And why wouldn't it be?

Abby yawned and stretched. She couldn't believe she'd woken up thinking about this stuff. She stumbled out of bed and pulled on the jeans she'd worn yesterday, grabbed a shirt from her dresser. Looking at herself in the mirror, she blinked a few times. Who was this person with a million animal facts clogging up her brain? And what was she doing in Abby's body?

"I'm going to take a walk," she told her mother at the breakfast table, slurping the last bit of milk from her bowl. "Get some exercise."

Her mother's expression was a complicated mix of worry and relief. "Exercise! Great! Now, where are you going to walk, exactly?"

Abby shrugged. "Just around the neighborhood. Nowhere special."

On her way out, she grabbed her jacket from the hall closet, in case it was chilly. She didn't really know where she was going. The Bentons'? The field across the street? She really just wanted to—well, what? Stop thinking for a while, maybe. Her head had become a zoo of strange animal facts, and last night she'd actually dreamed she was rowing a canoe down a river and looking for moose. She was pretty sure that wasn't a normal dream for an eleven-year-old girl to have.

The sky was so blue, Abby thought about going back inside for her camera so she could take a picture of it. Only she thought maybe if you took a picture of an all-blue sky, it wouldn't capture the beauty, just the blueness, and it might as well be a picture of a blue wall. It might depress you later, to look at your blue sky picture, because what you would be remembering was something grand, and what you would actually see in the picture was not grand at all, just flat and lifeless.

So she continued on across the street to the empty lot that wasn't empty at all, of course, enjoying the rambling nature of her thoughts. She liked the sensation of her mind running free in one direction, then another. Her beach chair was still parked behind the large oak, but it was damp from the morning air, so Abby walked through the weeds, thinking about how she should draw a map of the lot, show where all the trees were located, and the wisteria vines and the hydrangeas that sat on the edges of where the house used to be. They seemed to Abby to be waiting patiently, as though they expected the house to come back any minute.

Maybe she could do more than a map. Maybe she could actually build a model of the lot and make a house—out of a cardboard box or balsa wood, something light and easy to glue—to put on the lot, the house she'd build if the lot was hers. She could take pictures and do sketches in her drawing notebook and make lists of all the plants and the trees and the birds that had settled there after the house had been torn down. Maybe she would see the fox again and take its picture too. And then she'd figure out what she needed to build models of the trees and the flowers, the birds and the fox. Sculpey clay, pipe cleaners, toothpicks, paper clips—what else? What could she use for flowers? Tissue paper?

Clapping her hands as she ran, she headed back to her house to get her drawing supplies and her camera. Her mind bloomed with a dozen more ideas—maybe she could make furniture for the house, and maybe she could—

Abby froze in the middle of the street.

Kristen and Georgia were sitting on her front steps.

Abby's heart thudded in her chest and a strange

roaring filled her ears. Her mind, which had been running along at fifty miles an hour just a second before, came to a complete halt. She couldn't think of what to do, so she just stood there, half wishing a car would come whizzing down the road and hit her—just barely—so she could be whisked off in an ambulance to a faraway hospital.

"Hey, Abby, we were hoping you'd be back soon!" Kristen called out. "Your mom said we could wait for as long as we wanted."

Abby opened her mouth. Nothing came out. *This must be a bad dream*, she told herself, *the kind where you try to scream, but you don't make a sound.*

Abby's mother peeked out the front door. "Oh, good! You're back," she called cheerfully. "Look who's here!"

Abby took a deep breath and ordered herself to say something. "I see."

Abby's mother frowned. Clearly, Abby was not excited enough. "I think it's awfully nice of Kristen and Georgia to come by. It's such a beautiful morning."

Which has now been totally ruined, Abby

thought as she forced herself to cross the street and straggle up the sidewalk toward her front steps. "What do you want?" she asked, looking at Kristen.

Kristen smiled brightly. "Just to talk, Abby. You haven't been hanging around much lately. To be honest, we've been sort of concerned."

"Kristen says you've stopped eating lunch with them," Abby's mom reported, coming out onto the porch. "She's worried about you. So is Georgia."

"No, they aren't," Abby said. She stood in front of them, wondering if she could get up the steps without one of them grabbing her ankle and pulling her down. "They really aren't."

Kristen's mouth dropped open. "God, Abby, how can you say that? You're one of my best friends."

"Mine too," Georgia offered unconvincingly. "I've been totally worried about you."

Abby sat down on the bottom step. She thought she might be having an out-of-body experience, and sitting down was probably the best thing to do.

"We just think maybe something's wrong," Kristen explained, turning to look up at Abby's mom. "Sometimes that happens when kids start middle school. They change. Like, Abby has completely stopped hanging out with us, and she's friends with some really weird kids. And I'm sorry, Abby"—and now she turned to face her—"but Anoop Chatterjee? Jafar Ross? Please."

Georgia let out a dramatic sigh. "Let's go, Kristen. Abby's just not interested in being friends with us anymore."

"Wait!" Her mother held up her hand, as though ordering the girls to stop. "Abby, these are your best friends, and they care about you. The three of you should go upstairs and talk. I just pulled a tray of carrot muffins out of the oven. Why don't I bring some up?"

"C'mon, let's talk, Abby," Kristen echoed Abby's mother. "We want to help you."

Abby followed Kristen and Georgia upstairs to her room, like it was their house and not hers. Like she was the intruder. She took a deep breath and reminded herself that she wasn't against anyone, not even Kristen and Georgia.

"Nice place you've got here," Kristen said as she looked around at the mess Abby had left that morning. "Clean it much?"

Abby took a seat on her unmade bed. She made her voice sound friendly. Cheerful. "Why are you here?"

"We're concerned about you, didn't you hear?" Georgia asked in a nasal voice, Georgia being prone to allergies in the fall. Once she'd sneezed during a gymnastics meet and fell off the balance beam. Remembering this now, Abby almost laughed, but she didn't. She didn't want to be like them, laughing at things people couldn't help, like sneezing at the wrong time or being a terrible runner.

So instead of laughing, she looked at Georgia and said, "You should be friends with people who actually like you instead of just use you." She pulled her stuffed leopard, Perd, out from under her pillow and stroked him on his spotted head. "You'd probably be a lot happier."

Georgia shook her head, either in disgust or sheer disbelief. "When did you get so weird? Are you on drugs?"

"Enough." Kristen pulled out Abby's desk chair, turned it so it was facing the center of the room, took a seat. "You're both so totally immature sometimes. Of course Abby isn't taking drugs. She's just going through a difficult stage." She smiled a snaky, grown-up smile. "She'll grow out of it."

Then she leaned toward Abby, face serious, like a concerned camp counselor. "So what's up, Abby? We're all really worried about you. On top of everything, you look like you're getting fatter. You're going to cross the line into Christine Boggs territory if you're not careful."

Christine Boggs was famously fat. While Abby was officially chubby, even "had issues with her weight," as her mother would put it when her concern about Abby's weight was at its peak, Christine was obese, and she walked through school with her head down. Abby didn't think she'd ever seen Christine look at another human being.

Little waves of shame began to slap at her ankles. She clutched Perd and looked at her thighs. They reminded her of bread dough. She glanced at her stomach, where a roll of fat peeked over the waistband of her jeans.

She tried to think about something else. She tried to think about the house she was going to build, and how she could make the birds look like they were really flying. With wires, maybe? Or else the birds could sit in the hydrangea bushes, their wings spread, like they'd just landed.

Abby glanced out the window, wondering if the fox was across the street. It could be looking up at her right this very second. Suddenly she knew that the fox was *definitely* across the street and *definitely* trying to tell her something. *Don't listen to them, Abby*, the fox was calling. *Don't listen!*

I won't! Abby called back in her mind.

She turned to Kristen. "I'm on a diet," she lied, clutching Perd so Kristen couldn't see her hands trembling. "I've already lost two pounds."

Kristen smiled a great big fake smile. "That's great! You should come walk with us at lunchtime. We've started doing laps around the blacktop."

"That's a great idea," Abby said, smiling her own fake smile. "Maybe I will."

Her mother tapped on the door. "I've got muffins!" she exclaimed, carrying a tray into the room. "Oh, Abby, your desk is such a mess! Where am I going to put this?"

Kristen cleared off the desktop and took the tray from Abby's mother. "These look delicious, Mrs. Walker," she said. "You're the best cook!"

"Why, thank you, Kristen," Abby's mother said, clearly pleased. "You know, I wish you'd come over more often. I was so happy when you and Abby started spending time together last spring."

"Me too," Kristen said. "In fact, I'm going to come pick up Abby on Monday so we can walk to the bus stop together. We haven't spent enough time together lately."

Abby's mother beamed. "That sounds wonderful."

Kristen turned to Abby. "See you at seven fifty Monday morning?"

But she wasn't smiling anymore.

On Monday, Abby left the house at seven o'clock and walked the three miles to school.

Chapter Seventeen

abby had spent three lunch periods in the computer lab, and she wasn't getting anywhere. There was too much information! How could there be so much written about the Columbian ground squirrel? It was ridiculous! At this rate, it would take the rest of the year for her to get through the first five animals on Mrs. Benton's list. But she knew Mrs. Benton and Anders wanted something soon. They hadn't actually given her a deadline, but Abby couldn't help feeling like she should work as fast as she could.

She punched the print button and walked over to the printer on the table next to Mr. Gruber's desk. Two measly pages of notes shot out onto the tray. She collected them, knowing they weren't enough, but she'd sworn to herself that she'd take something—*anything*—to the Bentons' today. At least they would know she was trying.

Suddenly she was aware of someone looking over her shoulder. Marlys Barry was standing behind her, reading the page in Abby's hand.

"'Pronghorn deer'?" Marlys raised an eyebrow. "That sounds weird."

Abby hugged the pages to her chest. "It's not really any of your business," she snapped.

"I didn't say it was my business. Except that I know a lot about animals, but I've never heard of a pronghorn deer before."

"You're interested in animals?"

"Sure," Marlys said with a toss of her head. "I'm going to be a vet, aren't I?"

Like I'm supposed to know that, Abby thought. Still, this was interesting information. Marlys liked animals, Marlys spent a lot of time on the computer. . . .

"Do you like to do research on animals?" Abby asked in a bright tone of voice.

"Sometimes, I guess. Why?" Marlys sounded suspicious.

Should Abby ask for Marlys's help? How the heck could she explain the whole story? It would take forever, and Marlys might think she was crazy. *You're helping some man you hardly even know to write a poem? About the Lewis and Clark expedition? So he'll want to keep living?*

It did sound weird. *Was* weird. Abby still couldn't figure out how she'd gotten herself into it. It had something to do with the fox, she thought, and Wallace, and Anders. Something about Anders made Abby want to help him—after all, he'd helped her with no questions asked when she was making her getaway from Kristen and Georgia.

"No reason," Abby said, deciding that her reasons for what she was doing were too complicated to make sense to anybody but herself. She walked back to her desk and shoved the pages into her notebook.

As she walked up the hill toward the Bentons' farm that afternoon, she kept thinking that maybe she should turn around. She'd have at least another page of notes by the end of the week. Showing up with only two pages might make it seem like she didn't really care—and she *did* care! She'd just been given a job she wasn't that good at, that was all.

Mrs. Benton's face was full of expectation when she opened the front door. "What have you got there?" she asked, nodding toward the folded-up pages Abby held clutched in her hand. "Something for Matt?"

"It's not much." Abby wondered again if she should have come. She unfolded the sheets of paper and tried to smooth out the wrinkles. "I haven't had very much time to work on the list you gave me. It's been a pretty busy week. See, we have this holiday chorus thing we're doing in December and—"

"Why don't you show Matt what you've got?" Mrs. Benton took Abby by the arm and pulled her into the house. Lowering her voice, she added, "He could use a little cheering up today. He's feeling low. Won't say why." Increasing her volume, she called, "Matt, Abby's here!"

Matt was sitting on the couch in front of the TV, which was on, but the sound was so low you could hardly hear it. "Hey, Abigail," he greeted her listlessly. He patted the cushion beside him. "Have a seat. I'm watching some cooking show. You ever make your own corn dogs?"

Abby tentatively made her way to the couch. "Um, I can't really stay. I just wanted to give you some notes I wrote about some of the Lewis and Clark animals. For your poem."

Matt, eyes still glued to the TV, held out his hand. "Notes, huh? Well, let me see 'em."

Abby handed him the pages, her face hot. Would he throw them to the floor, yell, *You call these notes?*

Matt slowly sat up and reached for the remote. Turning off the TV, he leaned forward, reading what Abby had given him. He read the first page, then slipped it behind the second and kept reading. Finally he looked at Abby. "Can you imagine what it was like for Lewis and Clark? Imagine walking down your street and tripping over some animal you'd never seen before. Wouldn't that be cool?"

Abby nodded, thinking of the fox. Of course, she hadn't discovered foxes, but then again, Lewis and Clark hadn't really discovered pronghorn deer, either. The Indians had probably known about them for thousands of years. But when you saw an animal right in front of you, one you'd never seen before in your entire life, well, it was pretty amazing. It made you wonder what else was waiting to be discovered.

Matt folded the pages into a neat square and tucked them into his shirt pocket. "This was really nice of you to do, Abigail. Really nice. To be honest, I'd kind of gotten stuck, and I was feeling pretty down about it. It means a lot to me that you'd go to this trouble."

"It's not very much," Abby told him, feeling guilty. He was making such a big deal when she'd hardly done anything at all. "I'm going to do more. In fact, I'm going to ask my mom if I can use her computer tonight."

Matt patted Abby's shoulder. "You've done plenty. I really appreciate it."

"Anders is mucking out the stalls if you'd like to say hello," Mrs. Benton said, smiling at Abby as though the last few minutes had pleased her considerably. "I'm sure he'd like to see you. Seems all he talks about lately is 'Abby this' and 'Abby that.'"

"You've got a fan, that's for sure," Matt said with a nod.

Abby didn't know what to say. She'd never had a fan before. "I guess I'll go find him. I could help him, uh—"

"Muck," Mrs. Benton supplied. "A clumsy-sounding word meaning 'dig manure with a pitchfork.' Builds character."

Abby could hear Anders humming to himself when she reached the barn. Standing just outside of the barn door, she called out "Hey," hoping that Anders would come out to see her. She didn't want to take a chance of getting too close to a horse. "I just stopped by for a little while. I gave your dad some animal notes."

Anders shuffled out of a stall, a pitchfork in his hand, wearing rubber boots that went up to above his knees. "That's great! That's amazing! So you showed them to Matt already?"

Abby nodded. "They sort of cheered him up,

I think." She pointed to Anders's pitchfork. "Do you mind having to do that? Mucking out stalls, I mean?"

"At first the smell got to me, but now I like it. I mean, I know it's poop and everything, but it's not like dog poop, which in my opinion really stinks. Horse manure, I don't know. It has this kind of comforting smell. I guess that sounds weird. My mom says I'm getting weirder now that I'm being homeschooled. She thinks I should move to Virginia and live with her. I'll be less weird that way."

"My mom thinks I'm fat," Abby offered. "She doesn't say it, though. Not directly. She says I have issues with my weight."

"But you're not fat!" Anders exclaimed. He looked outraged. "You're exactly right!"

Abby, feeling pleased, tried to return the compliment. "Well, I don't think you're weird. So I guess our moms are wrong, huh?"

"I guess so." Anders grinned, then motioned in the direction of the stalls with his pitchfork. "The horses are all out in the pasture, if you wanted to help me clean the stalls. I'm only allowed to work in here if the horses are out. Matt's worried I'll get kicked in the head." He rolled his eyes.

Abby followed Anders into the barn. She liked the thought of being the kind of girl who mucked out stalls. Who hung out in a barn. Back when she was trying to make Kristen and Georgia believe she was an expert equestrian, she'd read tons of novels about horses—*Black Beauty*, *Misty of Chincoteague*, *The Black Stallion*—and stories about girls who had horses that they loved more than anything else. Abby had pretended she was that sort of girl, a horsey girl, but what she really liked to imagine was her imaginary horse's stall, with all its hooks holding well-oiled pieces of equipment, and the clean, sweet-scented straw on the ground.

"You're right, you do get used to the smell, don't you?" Abby called over the stall wall to Anders a few minutes later, scooping a load of manure onto her pitchfork. "It's really not that bad."

"I'd like to make it into a perfume, or an after-shave, wouldn't you?" Anders called back. He paused, and then said, "Now you have to admit, *that* makes me sound weird."

Abby giggled. "Yeah, sort of. But it's a good sort of weird."

Another pause. "There's a good sort of weird?"

"Yeah," Abby said. "I'm pretty sure there is. Don't you think there is?"

"I hope so," Anders replied. "It would sure make my life a whole lot easier."

That night Abby sat at her mom's computer and typed "mule deer" into the search engine box. All during dinner, she couldn't stop thinking about how grateful Matt had been that she'd helped him with his research. And the more she thought about that, the more she thought about Matt—what was going on with him exactly? He'd been in the army, he'd served in Iraq, and now he was raising bees and blueberries on his mom's farm. And he was depressed—or mentally ill. Maybe he had that sickness that soldiers got after they'd been in combat, where they couldn't shake the war off their shoulders.

Abby leaned back in her chair. She wished she could ask Matt what was wrong with him, but she knew she couldn't. You just didn't ask people things like that. But she wanted to know—she *needed* to know.

She sat up straight. Deleted "mule deer" from the search engine box. Typed in "Matt Benton, soldier, Iraq War."

And watched as the results tumbled down the screen.

Chapter Eighteen

the fox hid in the bushes a few feet away from the chicken coop. Watching. She was just watching. She thought if she observed the chickens long enough, she would grow to like them, and if she liked them, she wouldn't want to eat them.

It was a theory, anyway.

She'd only eaten two mice this week. And a vole. She'd turned her nose up at the sparrows flitting across her field. Mere children. She did not eat children. She had a line she wouldn't cross. No children. And now: no chickens.

It was the noise of the killing she'd lost her taste for, the violent screeches and squawks. On the nights when she'd avoided mice and moles and voles, dining instead on berries and weeds, her dreams weren't as bad. She dreamed of other stories, old stories, stories of crossing the raging river over the spine of a fallen tree, or bundling her kits into the safety of a dank cave. Some nights, when all she'd had to eat was wild grasses, she dreamed of Crow, her old friend.

She wondered now if Abby was in the field. Sometimes the girl spent the entire afternoon in an old chair behind the wide oak, drawing in a notebook, writing things down. The fox had watched, envious. If only she could write things down! She could write down all the stories, especially the ones that had kept her awake at night. She would carry them with her in her teeth, instead of in her head.

A brown-and-orange chicken came to the edge of the coop and clucked a worried cluck. The fox sighed and trotted back into the woods. She would not scare the chickens. She would not eat them.

It was midafternoon. A flock of wrens had

settled into the trees and were now chirping gaily to one another, making their plans to fly south in a few weeks. They quieted when they noticed the fox, then burst back into excited chatter after she'd moved out of sight. The fox sighed again. Had she really been that bad? Was every little creature afraid of her now?

The fox shook off the feeling that the whole world was afraid of her—a ridiculous notion— and tried to concentrate on how best to help Abby. No more baring of her teeth, she decided. But there must be something she could do to keep the raccoon girls away once and for all. They were sneaky girls, nosing around Abby's yard when they thought no one was looking. What did they hope to find? the fox wondered. Weapons? Abby locked in the teeth of a snare trap?

Perhaps she should talk to that dog. The hound. Once the fox had tried to track him, only to find that the hound was on *her* trail. Disconcerting, to say the least. For a hound, he was quiet, covert. He knew things. Should the fox cross the creek and find him?

She had to admit she found the idea frightening. She'd spent more than one night up a tree, pinned there by a baying dog hoping to snag her in his teeth the minute she fell out.

Still. The hound seemed an intelligent sort. Reasonable. Maybe he knew something about humans that she didn't. Oh, she knew a lot. Maybe too much. But she didn't know much about helping them. She'd never tried it before.

She'd ask the hound. She'd make herself.

And if he tried to eat her for dinner, she'd tell him about the chickens, how her mouth had watered just looking at them. How she'd walked away.

Chapter Nineteen

thursday, after she'd finished eating her lunch, Abby sat down at the computer next to Marlys's. She carefully laid out Mrs. Benton's list of animals to the right of her keyboard, the side closest to Marlys, and next to it she put the article she'd printed out from her mom's computer the night before. FIVE U.S. SOLDIERS KILLED IN ATTACK ON BASE IN IRAQ, the headline read, followed by the subhead, ONE MIRACULOUSLY SURVIVES TRUCK BOMBING.

Abby logged on to her school account. She

checked her library page and discovered she had two overdue books. The only new e-mail in her in-box was from Anoop, reminding her that the Science Club's Rocket Fair was next weekend. She read the e-mail several times while glancing at Marlys, waiting for her to sneak a peek at her papers.

She felt rather than saw Marlys reading, and then she heard a little *hmmm* escape from her lips. What would Marlys make of it? She'd never be able to put the two pages together, the war story and the list of weirdly named animals. She'd *have* to ask.

Wait for it, Abby told herself, *wait for it. . . .*

Marlys tapped on her shoulder. "I know it's none of my business—"

Abby shook her head, as though she'd been startled from her thoughts. "Huh? I'm sorry, were you asking me a question?"

Marlys pointed to the Iraq article. "Is that for a project or something?"

"Or something," Abby said with a shrug. "Well, it's definitely a project, but it's not a school project. It's this project I'm doing for a friend."

"*For* a friend? Do you mean *with* a friend?"

"Well, it's sort of both, actually. For and with."

Marlys scratched her nose. She sniffed, then clucked her tongue a couple of times. "Do you mind me asking what kind of project?"

Abby drew her finger along the part of the headline that read ONE MIRACULOUSLY SURVIVES TRUCK BOMBING. "That soldier? The one who survived? I know him. And he's writing a poem. About animals. And I'm helping him by looking up stuff about the animals."

"Interesting," Marlys said, scratching her nose again. "So that's why you're coming in here every day?"

Abby nodded.

"But you don't like to." Marlys reached over and plucked Mrs. Benton's list from Abby's desk. "I mean, you're really terrible at it, anyway. I hear you moaning and groaning to yourself, and you've hardly gotten any material. What did you print out the other day? Two pages? That's pretty lame."

"I'm the worst person at research in the world," Abby agreed. "I'm totally pathetic."

Marlys shook her head. She appeared to think something over. "Fine," she declared finally. "I'll help you. My cousin is in the army. He's been to Afghanistan three times so far. And I happen to know a lot about animals."

"You're going to be a veterinarian," Abby reminded her. "You'd have to know a lot."

Marlys looked at Mrs. Benton's list. "Have you done the California newt yet?" she asked, already typing.

"Not yet," Abby replied cheerfully, stretching her arms over her head. Wow, talk about being on easy street! Now she'd have pages and pages of research to bring Matt.

Marlys smacked the back of Abby's chair. "Well, you Google it too," she grumbled. "I'll help you, but you need to learn how to do this stuff. You'll never get into college if you don't."

After lunch, Abby went to her locker to get her science notebook. Some kids standing across the hall snickered when they saw her, and Abby wanted to tell them to shut up. Didn't they know there was a war going on? When she clicked open her combination and saw the pink yogurt smeared all over her books, she turned, and sure enough, now they were doubled over with laughter.

"Enjoy your lunch!" one of the boys called out, and a new burst of hilarity erupted.

Abby stood very still. She'd been so caught up in her research for Matt, she'd almost forgotten about Kristen and Georgia. Had practically forgotten they existed. Well, this was one big honking reminder, wasn't it?

Why did they care so much? The question played over and over in her head as she walked to the bathroom to get paper towels. Why did they care? Why did they care? She hadn't done anything to them, hadn't hit them or spit on them or talked behind their backs. All she'd done was walk away from their lunch table.

How pathetic, Abby thought as she wiped the yogurt off her Spanish book. Was this the best they could do? She herself could think of a hundred worse things. If they really wanted to get her, they could make a website where they could write mean things about her, they could spread rumors that Abby was retarded or had kissed a lot of boys behind the school. They could trap her in the bathroom and make her drink toilet water.

Really, Kristen and Georgia appeared to be total amateurs when it came to making someone's life miserable. Still, Abby decided she'd better keep an eye on them. Who knew what lame-brain scheme they'd come up with next? Banana peels on the gym floor, or shaving cream in Abby's backpack. Kindergarten stuff.

Medium girl stuff, Abby decided. Boring, run-of-the-mill medium girl stuff. But a thought nagged at her as she hurried to science class— what if they were working up to something really terrible?

She watched the medium girls' table at lunch the next day, half paying attention as Anoop and Jafar discussed next year's World Cup prospects. Not knowing anything about international soccer—*football*, Anoop insisted she call it—Abby was free to observe what Kristen and Georgia were doing. Nothing, it appeared.

Kristen was peeling the crust off her sandwich, and Georgia was blowing into a straw wrapper and sucking the air back really quickly to make the straw collapse. Bess and Myla were rolling a grape back and forth to each other across the table. Casey was reading *The Hunger Games*, and it looked like Rachel was doing homework.

Mostly it just looked boring over at the medium girls' table. It didn't seem like anyone was plotting some mastermind scheme against her. Abby bet that Bess, Myla, Rachel, and Casey didn't even care anymore. Come to think of it, Myla had even smiled at her in language arts the other day. A regular, nice-to-see-you sort of smile, with nothing hiding behind it.

Abby wondered what would happen if she went over to the medium girls' table right now. Maybe Bess, Myla, Rachel, and Casey would make room for her, kick Kristen and Georgia out.

Or maybe they'd all sigh with relief. At last they would have someone to be mean to again!

Abby decided to stay put.

"Why do you suppose this Anders cannot

cross the creek?" Anoop asked suddenly, examining a baby carrot as though he wasn't sure it was worth eating. "Do you think his parents fear him drowning?"

Abby turned her attention back to her friends. She'd told Anoop and Jafar about the Bentons at the beginning of the lunch period, secretly hoping they'd be intrigued enough to join her and Marlys in their research, but they'd only seemed half-interested at the time, and Abby had dropped the subject. Now she could see that Anoop had been mulling it over in his careful way as he'd discussed soccer with Jafar and munched on his daily *dosas*.

"It's not that kind of creek," Abby told him. "It's only about four feet wide and six inches deep. But he says it's beyond the safe perimeters, whatever that means. I think his dad's worried that he'll get lost if he crosses it."

"Maybe his dad thinks he'll get kidnapped," Jafar added, a gleam in his eye. "By pirates. Are there many pirates in your neighborhood, Abby?"

Abby laughed. "Oh, yeah. Tons."

"My grandmother is very frightened of water," Anoop told them. "She once fell off a ship. This is true. She was traveling from India to England to attend university. Just as the boat was pulling out from the dock, Grandmother leaned over to wave to her sister, and she fell into the water. She had on heavy clothes and was sure she would sink to the bottom, but a kind sailor saved her."

"So no crossing the creek for you," Jafar teased.

"Probably not," Anoop agreed, crunching on his carrot. "We don't even go to the swimming pool in our subdivision."

He lifted the flap on his lunch bag, peeked in, and shook his head sadly. "My lunch is all down-hill from here, I am afraid. Perhaps we should go visit this Marlys who is helping with the animals. We might be able to offer some assistance."

Jafar looked confused. "I thought we were going to play soccer."

"Football," Anoop corrected him. "And there will be time for that. But I am interested in Abby's project."

"Really?" Jafar tilted his head. "How come?"

Anoop reddened. "Because it is Abby's project."

Jafar seemed to consider this. "Okay," he said after a couple of seconds. "Let's go."

Abby trailed her friends out of the cafeteria. She would never go back to the medium girls' table, no matter how much yogurt they smeared in her locker. She wouldn't go back if Kristen and Georgia apologized for how mean they'd been to her and *begged* her to come back. She, Abigail Walker, was good with Anoop and Jafar, good with *dosas*, good with long conversations about soccer-that-you-had-to-call-football.

She was good with just the way things were.

marlys, it turned out, was an obsessive note taker. The next time Abby took notes to the Bentons' farm, she carried them in a three-ring binder.

"I hope I'm not giving him too many details," Marlys had told her on Monday, handing over a folder with at least twenty typed pages. "Let me know if I'm overwhelming him. Because he sounds like a person who could be overwhelmed pretty easily."

Abby worried about this too when she handed Matt the binder, which contained

Anoop and Jafar's notes too. Anoop's notes were carefully outlined and included illustrations, and Jafar's had peanut butter spots on them but were surprisingly thorough. There were three new pages of Abby's notes, and she thought she was getting better at sifting out the important information from the stuff that didn't matter so much.

Marlys, on the other hand, had practically written a book.

"I could tell her not to write so much," she told Matt as he took the pages from her. "She's just really into animals."

Matt had been sitting at the kitchen table. He looked more focused than the last time Abby had seen him, less sad. "I want to know everything," he assured her. "All the varieties, all the different facts. You think about what it must have been like way back then, when Lewis and Clark went exploring. It must have been so clean. So . . . so—"

"New?" Abby suggested, remembering what Anders had told her.

"New!" Matt exclaimed. "Yes, new! Untouched.

Just incredibly peaceful. I like to think of the animals walking around in the middle of all that peace."

Abby didn't think it was a good time to mention some of the interesting facts she'd been learning about predators and attacks on nests and mama bears, facts that didn't sound peaceful at all to her. So she just nodded.

"It's peaceful here, Mattie," Mrs. Benton called from the living room, where she was watching TV and untangling bridles. "Peaceful in the here and now. When are you going to believe that?"

"When I believe it, Ma," he called back, and then grinned at Abby. "She won't get off my case. Nag, nag, nag."

"I heard that!" Mrs. Benton yelled. Then in a voice more suited to the indoors, she called, "Abby, Matt's got a new list tacked to the wall behind the couch in here. He thinks it's great that you kids are helping out, don't you, son?"

Matt nodded. "Couldn't do it without you," he said, sounding distracted as he read through Abby's pages. "These notes look great, Abigail."

Anders was in the living room, sunk down in a puffy blue easy chair with a book in his lap. He held up it up so Abby could see. *Prairie Dogs: Community and Communication in an Animal Society.* "It's pretty interesting," he told her. "It's like prairie dogs live in this world of their own. Kind of like me."

"You're in your own world?" Abby asked him. "Anders World? Like Disney World?" She smiled, to show him she was teasing, but his expression stayed serious.

"Sort of. I mean, I don't know any other kids who live like this, do you?"

Abby pretended she didn't know what he meant. "A lot of kids are homeschooled around here. There's a bunch in my neighborhood."

Anders shut his book. "Yeah, but—"

"But they don't have to put up with their cranky grandmother all the livelong day, do they?" Mrs. Benton cut in.

"Yeah," Anders agreed. He tilted his head toward the kitchen. "Or—"

"He'll get better," Abby said, even though she had no idea whether Matt would get better or not. "Just wait and see. And then your life will be totally normal."

Anders didn't look 100 percent convinced.

Abby walked over to the couch and scanned the bits and pieces of paper stuck to the wall above it, looking for Matt's new list. Anders came and stood beside her.

"Sometimes I wish we had a computer we could use for our research," he told Abby. "Only, if we had a computer, I don't think Matt would put everything on the wall. And having everything on the wall is pretty interesting. I mean, look at this," he said, pointing to a drawing captioned *"Lepus townsendii campanius—white-tailed jackrabbit."* "Matt drew that. Isn't that cool?"

Abby nodded, imagining the walls of her room covered with pictures of the birds and weeds that lived across the street, each with its Latin name written underneath. Latin names were dignified, she decided. Every weed deserved one.

She found Matt's new list and pulled it down. *Carolina parakeet, Clark's nutcracker, meadowlarks, Mississippi kite*, the list began. Birds! She turned to Anders. "We're doing birds now!"

She stood a little taller, sucked in her gut. If anybody knew about birds, it was Abigail Walker. She was practically an expert.

"There are rodents on that list too," Matt called out. "And I want to know everything! No stinting on the details!"

"I promise," Abby called back cheerfully. "We won't!"

"He definitely likes the details," Abby assured Marlys on the phone that afternoon when she got home, so it wasn't surprising when Abby, Anoop, and Jafar found her in the computer lab the next day after they finished eating, printing out page after page on the black-tailed prairie dog.

"They don't hibernate," Marlys told them. "Most prairie dogs do, but not the black-tailed prairie dog. Isn't that weird? Now I'm trying to find out why that is."

"It's a rodent!" Jafar exclaimed, reading over

her shoulder. "Order: Rodentia; it says so right there. I thought it would be a dog."

"It looks like a rather large rat to me," Anoop said. "Possibly more attractive."

Marlys laughed. When she laughed, Abby thought Marlys looked like an entirely different person. First of all, she had dimples when she laughed, and her eyes crinkled in a nice way and looked much bluer than they did when she was just sitting in front of a computer or walking down the hallway. Abby could see that one day Marlys would probably be pretty, even if she wasn't pretty right now. You could just tell with some people. You could see their faces' futures.

"You want to come with me to my locker?" Abby asked her. She was asking because she didn't want to be in the hallway alone during lunch period. But she was also asking because she thought it would be nice to be friends with another girl again. She thought she might be ready.

"Let me just get all this stuff together." Marlys began gathering the pages the printer had pushed out into a neat stack. She looked up at Abby. "Would you mind going to the bathroom first? I need to floss."

"Floss?" Abby had never heard of anyone flossing in the girls' room before.

Marlys went red. "It's a promise I made my dad, that I would floss after every meal. He just spent the last year getting ten crowns on his teeth because he never flosses. So now he's kind of obsessed with it."

"You could just tell him you flossed," Jafar suggested. "I mean, how's he going to find out that you didn't?"

"I have to take him the used floss," Marlys admitted. "Yeah, I know. Gross. But, like I said, he's obsessed."

"It's nice that he cares," Abby said sympathetically.

Marlys smiled. "Yeah, I guess. He's a nice dad. He just has rotten teeth."

"Well, since we cannot join you in the bathroom, we will go see what is happening on the football field," Anoop said. "Come on, Jafar. I feel like showing Thomas how the game is played."

Abby and Marlys watched the two boys as

they left the computer lab. Marlys looked at Abby. "Football? Really?"

"Soccer," Abby explained. "Everybody else in the world but us calls it football."

Marlys sighed. "Boy, do I hate soccer. My parents made me start playing when I was three. I hate most sports. Except for baseball." She looked at Abby hopefully. "Do you like to play baseball?"

Abby thought about it. "I think I might," she said. "At least I'm pretty sure I don't hate it."

Marlys smiled. "That's good. That's a good place to start."

Chapter Twenty-One

no one was home after school, so Abby shoved a bunch of grapes into a bag and grabbed a sleeve of graham crackers from the pantry. She added a bottle of water and a book about animals she'd found in Gabe's room, and then she put everything in her backpack. Just as she was walking out the door, the phone rang.

"Ab? It's Dad. Can you bring some bottled water up to the office? The water guy was supposed to bring a new five-gallon thing today, but he never showed. Two bottles ought to do it."

Abby grabbed the water from the fridge and went out through the mudroom door and up the stairs to her dad's office. She hardly ever went up there because her dad didn't like to be disturbed while he was working, and besides, there was nothing fun to do—no TV, only one computer, and her dad was always using it. Her dad used to have a fish tank that Abby liked to look at, but some disease wiped out all the fish, so there wasn't even that anymore.

Dropping her backpack at the top of the stairs, she tapped on the door. "I've got your water, Dad."

"Come on in, Ab," her dad called. "I'm on the phone."

He was tipping back in his seat, his feet on the desk, wearing a headset. "Just put 'em on the desk, thanks," he whispered to Abby, nodding to the one spot not covered up in papers. "Oh, just my daughter, bringing me something to drink," he said into the little mic on his headset. "A man builds up a thirst after a long day of wheeling and dealing."

Abby rolled her eyes. Her dad developed and

marketed computer software. It wasn't exactly like he was some hotshot on Wall Street. Still, she thought it was sort of neat that he'd built his own business. Not just anybody could do that.

"Okay, thanks, Ab," her dad whispered, giving her a wave, like he was ready for her to go. She waved back and started to leave, but paused to look at the "rogues' gallery," as her dad called it, a collection of framed photographs of family and friends that took up most of the wall near the door. There was her dad when he was a high school football star, there were Grammy and Gramps on their wedding day. One picture showed Abby dressed up for Easter when she was two, another documented John and Gabe at the beach last summer, John buried up to his head in sand, Gabe with one foot on his chest.

Abby hadn't seen the beach pictures before. She smiled at the one of her mom sitting under a huge umbrella, a sombrero-size hat on her head, her nose smeared with zinc oxide. There was even one of her dad, which was rare, since he was the family photographer. But there he was, waist deep in the ocean, waving toward the shore.

But where was Abby? Abby scanned all the beach pictures and realized there wasn't one of her. In fact, there weren't any new ones of Abby at all. She looked and looked, but the most recent one of her was from fourth grade, and she was standing behind a chair, so you could only see the top part of her.

She looked over at her dad, who was laughing at something the person on the phone had just said. Did he even realize there were no new pictures of her? Was that a coincidence, or did he do it on purpose? Did he think, *No pictures of Abby in my rogues' gallery until she loses a little weight?*

Well, fine, just fine! Abby stuck her hands on her hips and glared at her dad, who wasn't paying the least bit of attention to her. Tears filled her eyes, and she swiped them away. Just fine! Be that way!

She turned back to the wall and grabbed a picture of herself, age four, on a pony. Then the Easter picture, and her third-grade school picture, and the one of her on Santa's lap when she was five. "Fine, fine, fine," she muttered to herself. "Just fine."

"Abby!" her dad hissed. "What on earth are you doing?"

She didn't answer. She grabbed one last picture—herself on the merry-go-round at the second-grade picnic—and stomped out of the office. Outside the door, she dumped all the pictures in her backpack.

"Be that way," she snarled at her father through the door. "See if I care."

Of course she cared. She knew that she cared. She'd care if somebody punched her in the gut, wouldn't she? Well, that's what her dad had done. He'd punched her in the gut. Didn't he know it would hurt?

How could someone not know that?

Outside, October had landed. Everything in the lot across the street was dying away, Abby knew that, but she also knew better. Seeds were everywhere. She couldn't walk five feet without being covered by hitchhikers and burrs, all

178

wanting a ride to somewhere else, to a good piece of dirt where next spring they'd take root.

The afternoon was cool, but not cold. It was perfect weather for something. But what? Abby put down her backpack and set up her chair. She took out a graham cracker and began to nibble on it. The weeds rustled quietly in the breeze. Abby felt herself fill up with—what? Helium, it felt like, or rays of light. She thought if she wasn't careful, she might start dancing in circles. She began to laugh. She twirled around a couple of times for good measure. She laughed harder, thinking about those pictures in her backpack. Who did her dad think he was, anyway? The fat police?

On the third twirl, slightly dizzy, she came face-to-face with Wallace. The helium feeling turned electric. "Is everything okay?" she asked.

Wallace stood still for a moment, as though he wanted to make sure he had her attention, and then turned and marched toward the fence at the back of the lot, his tail wagging high in the air. Abby felt like he was telling her to follow him, but why? Maybe Anders was waiting for her at the creek. Maybe something had happened on the farm? Abby grabbed her backpack and scurried after the hound.

By the time they reached the creek, Wallace had picked up the pace, and Abby had to run to keep up with him. Halfway up the hill to the field, she began to feel strange again, and she realized—wildly, impossibly—that the running didn't hurt so much anymore. Her lungs didn't feel red hot, her throat wasn't tight, she didn't want to throw up.

She wished she could tell Claudia! She wished Claudia were with her that very minute. Or Marlys. Someone who would take her hand and swing around with her, laughing at the craziness of Abby running up a hill and not feeling like she was about to die.

She was panting by the time she reached the farmhouse. Wallace, she noticed, was not. Wallace stood at the top of the porch steps, eyeing Abby calmly, as though he'd just taken a stroll around the yard.

"Show-off," Abby scolded him.

She tapped on the porch door. She waited for Mrs. Benton's loud "Come in!" or Anders's face at the window. She stood for a minute, two minutes. She turned to look at the driveway. The Impala was gone, but the pickup truck was there. Maybe they'd gone on a field trip. Or to Walmart.

She was about to leave when the front door clicked open behind her. Abby turned to see Matt standing in the doorway, shadowed by the screen door. "Anders had to go get his flu shot," he told her. "He should be back in a half hour or so, if you want to wait."

They left Matt by himself? She didn't think Mrs. Benton and Anders ever left Matt alone in the house for more than a few minutes. It seemed like a bad idea to Abby. What if Matt got really depressed all of the sudden? Or thought someone was coming after him?

"Do you want some company?" she asked, her face growing hot. Matt would think she was stupid for asking if he wanted some eleven-year-old girl's company. But what else was she supposed to do? She pressed on. "Because I don't know about you, but sometimes I don't like hanging out by myself. Sometimes I do, though. So, I mean, it's up to you."

Matt shrugged. "I'm okay. I saw my doctor today. I always feel good on the days I see my doc."

Abby looked at Wallace. Wallace looked at Abby.

"Maybe I'll just wait until they get back," she said. She peered toward the road, willing Mrs. Benton's car into sight. How could they have left Matt by himself?

Matt stepped out onto the porch. "You can stay if you want to, but you don't have to. I mean it, I'm good. I'll be okay. Everyone worries too much."

"Oh, I'm not worried at all," Abby said, talking over him, wanting to go, but feeling like she shouldn't. "What would I be worried about? I just want to wait for Anders. I've got, well, stuff—stuff I need to talk to him about."

Matt laughed. "I don't need a babysitter, Abigail."

Abby shoved her hands into her pockets and

rocked back on her heels. She felt dumb. Matt was an adult. He didn't need a kid to take care of him. But Matt wasn't like other adults, Abby reminded herself. He was more like a broken cup that had been glued back together. Maybe the glue would hold, maybe it wouldn't.

"I've been taking my meds and talking every day with my doctor at the VA," Matt went on. "I'm real steady right now. I'm getting better." He was quiet for a minute, then said, "You want to go see the horses? Long as you're here?"

Abby stared at him. Horses? He wanted to see the horses?

"My doc says I need to give the horses another chance." Matt reached over to pull a dry, brown leaf from a pot of geraniums on the porch railing, crumpling it between his fingers. "You know that horse, Ruckus? The one that girl Louise rides?"

Abby nodded.

"That's my horse. I got him around the same time I got Wallace. He's getting old, man. I used to ride him all the time."

"How come you stopped?"

Matt stared straight ahead. "When I was in Iraq—" He stopped. "It was just bad, okay? Some really bad stuff happened. And it wasn't about horses, but horses kind of trigger this feeling in me, this feeling like I can't control things, the way I couldn't control anything over there. That's what my doc says, anyway. I was really scared over there, Abigail. I mean, all the time. And mad. And—" Matt rubbed his eyes. "And a lot of things. A lot of junk. But I'm trying to get better."

He looked at Abby and smiled. "One day at a time, right, Abigail?"

Wallace led the way to the barn. Matt had a stiff-legged walk, like an old man, and Abby wanted to reach out and take his hand, help him along. She'd never felt this way about an adult before, like she was the one who was supposed to make sure everything was okay.

When they reached the door, Matt turned to Abby. "I've taken Ruckus out every day this week, doctor's orders, and he's been real steady. In fact, I'm thinking I might let Anders ride him." He paused before going on. "Because, like

I said, Ruckus is real steady. So if you wanted to ride him, you could. I've got an old Western saddle you could use."

"Oh, I don't know," Abby said in what she hoped was a breezy sort of tone. She couldn't believe Matt was offering to let her ride Ruckus. He was the one person she thought she was safe around when it came to horses. He should let Anders ride. Anders actually knew how, after all, unlike Abby. Well, even if Anders *was* allowed to ride one day, that didn't mean Abby had to get up on a horse. "I guess I'm not really in the mood to ride."

Matt put his hand on her shoulder. "There's nothing to be afraid of, Abigail. Ruckus won't run away with you." Then he smiled. "I'm *trusting* Ruckus not to run away with you. I'll hold on to the reins the whole time."

Abby started to shake her head. Really, what was it going to take to convince Matt she wasn't the sort of person who rode horses? He, more than anyone else, should get it. Horses were big, and people fell off them. Hadn't Matt kept Anders from riding for that very reason?

But he's trusting horses now, Abby told herself. *That's a big deal. That's totally opposite of where he was just a few weeks ago.* If she got up on Ruckus, it might help Matt get better. It might make him see that he had come to a safe place.

She thought about what she'd read in the article about the truck bombing. Imagined what it must have been like, to be blown into the air, flames all around you. How could you ever feel safe again after that? You'd have to work really hard at it, that was for sure. You'd have to come a long, long way.

Abby sucked in her gut. "I'm sort of scared of falling off," she announced in a voice louder than she intended. "But I guess I could try."

Matt nodded. "Trying is good."

Abby followed Matt into the tack room, paying close attention to everything he was telling her about riding as he searched around for a bridle: how to grip the saddle with her knees and hold the reins in one hand while her other hand was on the saddle horn. She tried to keep her breathing steady and her mind off the fact that all of the sudden she needed to go to the bathroom. Bad.

"I got Ruckus when I was just out of high school," Matt told Abby as they headed toward the horses' stalls, Matt carrying the saddle, Abby walking behind him holding the bridle, halter, and reins. "I actually thought I might go work on a ranch out west."

"Why didn't you?" Abby asked from the alley as Matt entered Ruckus's stall. Ruckus backed up a few steps when Matt threw the saddle on his back, and Abby did too.

"I joined the Peace Corps instead," Matt replied, patting Ruckus on the rump. "You're all right, boy," he told the horse. He leaned down to tighten the saddle's cinch strap around the horse's girth. He didn't sound nervous, but Abby could see his hands fumbling with the strap. "That's where I met Anders's mom, in Kenya. After we finished up with that, I joined the army. I'd done peace and thought I'd give war a try."

"Really?" What a weird thing to say!

Matt gave one last tug, then motioned for

Abby to hand him the halter and bridle. "No, not really." He laughed. "I joined the army so they'd pay for college when I was done. But I never got done. I stayed in. Anders was born in Germany, did he ever tell you that?"

Abby shook her head. She suddenly realized she didn't know much about Anders at all, like when his birthday was or what he liked to eat for dinner.

"Yeah, he was. We traveled all the time when we were over there. It was awesome." He slipped the halter over the horse's head, then gently pried open his mouth. Ruckus struggled, but finally allowed the bit to be inserted. Matt looked at Abby. "Okay, you ready to get up? Like I said, Ruckus is real easy. Nothing to be afraid of."

Abby wondered if he was saying that to try to convince her, or if he was trying to convince himself.

"I'm ready," she told him, though she didn't know if she was ready or not. When Matt boosted her up into the saddle, she settled into it and closed her eyes. She felt a little dizzy. "How many hands is Ruckus?" she asked, eyes still closed, not sure if she wanted to know the answer.

"Fifteen," Matt told her. "Pretty tall. Okay, I'm going to lead you guys out now. Hold on."

Abby held the reins in one hand and clung to the saddle horn with her other hand. Ruckus moved easily beneath her, his feet clopping against the wood floor. She supposed that compared to Matt, she seemed light to Ruckus. She straightened up and opened her eyes. Suddenly she had the strangest feeling, like maybe, for once, she was the right size.

"I'll lead you as long as you want me to," Matt said, taking the reins from Abby, "and then if you want to ride a little by yourself, you can. Just use the reins to let Ruckus know what direction you want to go in, and give him a little kick if you want him to go faster. You can just walk, though. You don't have to go any faster than this."

Abby sat up straight in the saddle and looked around her. Which made her want to lie down. She was up too high! The ground was miles beneath her, and if she fell, she'd break into a million pieces.

But you're not falling, she told herself, and she realized it was true. She wasn't even slipping. She gripped her knees tighter into Ruckus's sides, hoping she wasn't hurting him. But the horse clopped along, not seeming to give Abby a second thought.

I'm not falling, Abby thought gleefully. *I'm riding!*

Matt walked them into the field, turning around from time to time to look at Abby and smile. "You're doing great," he told her. "A natural."

Abby didn't feel like a natural exactly, but she didn't feel unnatural, either. She didn't feel like crying or throwing up or begging Matt to get her down. She felt—okay. Tall. She sat with this okay, tall feeling for a few minutes until she decided she wanted to feel something even bigger. "I guess I'd like to try to ride him by myself." Her voice sounded shaky. She tried again. "I'd like to ride him by myself."

Matt nodded slowly. "Uh, yeah, okay. You sure?"

Abby nodded, and Matt handed her back

the reins. "I'll just stay here in case you need me. Take as long as you want."

Abby tapped Ruckus gently on his side with her heel. He started off again in his slow-gaited walk. Abby took a deep breath and tapped his side again. She wanted more—not too much more, but more—and when Ruckus quickened into a trot, her stomach lifted toward her chest, the way it did when she swung high on the playground swings. *It's like flying*, she thought happily, though she knew they weren't even galloping. Who cared? You didn't have to go a hundred miles an hour in order to fly.

The helium feeling filled her up again as she and Ruckus trotted across the field, the October sun getting low in the sky. Abby threw her head back and laughed. She could do this forever. She never wanted to get off. She rode and rode and had no idea how long she'd been riding.

It was the thought of Matt standing alone in the field that made her turn back. When she reached him, he was crying. Abby's heart started beating hard. How could he be crying? Everything had been fine! He had been fine!

What had happened while she was gone? Did he think Ruckus had run off with her? Had thrown her?

"I'm okay!" Abby cried in a panicky voice. "I'm really okay! Everything's okay. Ruckus was steady, just like you said."

Matt shook his head, wiping his wet face with the back of his arm. "I know you're okay. Why wouldn't you be? You have everything ahead of you. Everything's new. And you think the world is beautiful."

"It is beautiful," Abby said, trying to sound calm even though her hands were shaking and she couldn't get her thoughts straight enough to figure out what she should do next. Did she need to call 911? *Simmer down*, she told herself. *Try to help*. To Matt, she said, "Look at Ruckus. He's beautiful, isn't he?"

Matt looked at Ruckus for a long time. "Yes," he said finally. "He really is."

Abby held out her hand to him. He reached up and took it.

"We could go inside and work on your poem until everyone gets back," Abby said, feeling better now that she had hold of him. "If you wanted to."

"Okay," he said, and to Abby he sounded like a little kid. She handed him the reins.

"He's real steady, just like you said," Abby repeated. "He's good. All you have to do is hold on."

Matt nodded. "I know."

They began walking toward the stable. "Do you know about George Shannon?" Abby asked, and when Matt shook his head, she said, "It's a really good story. You want to hear it?"

"Do I have a choice?" Matt asked with a laugh. He sounded better to Abby, more like a grown-up again.

"You don't," Abby told him. "So listen up."

Chapter Twenty-Two

where've you been?"

her mom called when Abby walked inside the house. "Dinner's almost ready."

"Just walking around the creek," Abby told her, coming into the kitchen, which smelled like onions and paprika.

"Could you stir the sauce for me?" Her mother was working on her laptop at the kitchen counter. "What creek, honey? I didn't know there was a creek around here."

"It's a couple streets over," Abby said, picking up the wooden spoon that was on the stove.

She stirred the liquid bubbling in the dutch oven. "It's not a very big creek, but it has some nice rocks."

Abby's mother looked up from the computer. "I didn't know you were interested in nature, honey. That's nice. And *I* have something nice to tell you."

Abby put down the spoon and took a seat at the kitchen table. Her mother's idea of nice and hers weren't always the same. She braced herself.

"Kristen has invited you to a sleepover at her house on Friday!" her mom announced, as though she were telling Abby she'd won the lottery. "You haven't slept over at Kristen's since last summer. And the other girls will be there too. Kristen was so excited when I told her you could come."

No way. No honking way. She'd wake up in the middle of the night with her sleeping bag filled with grasshoppers or ants, maybe both. They'd stick her finger in water while she was asleep to make her pee. Kristen would decide to do one of her famous "personality makeovers" and choose Abby as her victim, reciting a long list of Abby's faults and ways she could improve. Nope, Abby wasn't going.

But if she told her mom that, all the joy would drain out of her face. Her mom wanted so badly for everyone to be happy, for everything to work out. Maybe when your sister dies when you're nine, you spend the rest of your life trying to make sure nothing else bad happens, that no one's ever unhappy again. *But that's impossible*, Abby thought. *And unfair.*

It wasn't fair that Abby had to pretend things were nice all the time.

So she said it. Said, "I don't want to spend the night at Kristen's. The only reason I'm invited is so they can all gang up on me. They hate me."

"Of course they don't hate you!" her mom exclaimed. "How can you even think such a thing?" She walked over to the stove to stir the pot, then turned back to Abby. "Honey, I'm so sorry you feel this way, but it's simply not true."

Abby took a deep breath. "Listen to me, Mom. It *is* true."

Suddenly her mom looked angry. "Stop it! I

know you miss Claudia, I know it's hard when your best friend moves. But you have to make new friends, Abby. And here are these girls who seem like they're trying very hard to be friends with you. So why are you turning away? You need friends. Everybody needs friends. So whether you want to or not, you're going to this sleepover. You're going to make an effort to be nice."

Abby didn't know what to say. What do you do when you tell the truth and nobody believes you?

"I'm not going," she said after a few moments. "I'm really not."

Abby's mom sighed. "Do we need to talk to your father about this?"

Abby slumped in her chair. She knew her father would make her go. And while he was at it, he'd look her up and down and say something like, "You need more friends. You need to be outside, running around. That's how you lose weight."

"No," Abby replied glumly. "I guess not."

"You'll have a wonderful time, Abby!" Just

like that, her mom sounded like her old cheerful self again. Everything was happy, everyone was at peace. That was all that mattered.

Abby pushed back her chair and stomped out of the kitchen. She stomped up the stairs as loud as she could, each stomp announcing how mad she was, how irritated, how misunderstood. In her room, she flung herself on her bed and glared at Perd. "If I have to go, you're coming with me," she warned him.

Perd looked back at her, clearly dismayed.

Abby rolled over and reached to the floor beside her bed, where her copy of *Undaunted Courage* was lying open, facedown. Ha! Her mom hated when Abby mistreated books. "You'll crack the spine," she was always complaining.

"*You'll crack the spine,*" Abby hissed in a falsetto voice as she picked the book up. "*You'll crack the spine.*"

She lay back on the bed and tried to read. She still thought the book had too many boring parts, but she'd learned how to skim over them to get to the good stuff. She liked how brave the people on the Lewis and Clark expedition had been, traveling into unknown territory, trying to make friends with the Indians. And she liked thinking about George Shannon. She thought if she'd been on the expedition, they would have become friends. She wouldn't even have minded getting lost with him all the time. It would be like an adventure inside of an adventure.

"Abby, come down here! I want to talk to you!"

Her mom, Abby knew, was standing at the foot of the stairs, her hands on her hips. Abby had stomped off, and stomping wasn't really allowed in her house. It wasn't *nice*.

"You're going to that sleepover, Abby!"

Abby thought about George Shannon sitting all alone on the prairie, the coyotes howling in the distance.

Watch out, George, she wanted to call out. *They're getting closer.*

"Can't wait until tomorrow night!" Kristen chirped to her on the bus the next day.

Abby looked out the window. She looked at

the field, the once-green field now fading into brown. She wondered where the fox was. She looked at her hand, the skin perfectly smooth. She wondered if there'd been a fox at all.

"You are very quiet," Anoop told her at lunch. "Not that you are particularly noisy at other times. But today, you have hardly said a word."

Abby looked at him. She looked at Jafar. Could she tell them the truth? Would it make sense? It was worth a try, she supposed. Besides, she might as well find out if everyone thought she was crazy. "Would you believe me if I told you someone was out to get me?"

"You?" Jafar looked incredulous. "But you're nice."

"I would believe it," Anoop said.

"What?" Jafar exclaimed. "You're crazy!"

Anoop shrugged. "I know what I know. People are cruel, girls especially." He turned to Abby. "No offense. But I have noticed your friends no longer speak to you. Why is that?"

"Because I told them they weren't my friends," Abby admitted.

Anoop considered this. "Then can you

blame them for not speaking to you?"

"I guess not. But I wish they would just leave it at that."

"They have plans to hurt you?" Anoop looked concerned.

"I think so," Abby said. "I mean, maybe not physically. But they're going to do something to me. They've already smeared yogurt all over my locker. Who knows what they'll do next."

"Then let us help you."

"I don't think there's anything you can do," Abby told him, and then she laughed. She didn't know why she thought it was funny, but it was. She was eleven years old, a kid. Too young to have problems where no one could help. But what could she do if the only people who believed her were other kids?

Anoop looked confused, and Abby smiled at him. "If I think of anything you can do to help, I'll tell you," she assured him. "But for now I guess I just have to deal with it by myself."

Anoop nodded. "I understand."

When they met Marlys in the computer lab, they all took out their latest lists. Discoveries had been made. Jafar had learned that the wolverine had at least three other names: skunk bear, carcajou, and quickhatch. Marlys reported that the Western tanager was actually considered to be a member of the cardinal family and had been officially reassigned. It was not naturally red, but turned red from the bugs it ate, which in turn were red from the plants *they* ate.

As a rule of thumb, Anoop told them, stay away from grizzly bears.

They all nodded at this wisdom. Abby yanked a loose thread at the hem of her T-shirt. Could Matt be helped by knowing these things? Would it make him better? Really help him finish his poem?

Did it help just knowing someone wanted to help you, even if they couldn't, not really?

Abby looked at her friends. Her friends. Yes, she decided. It did. Later that afternoon, sitting behind the oak tree among the wild weeds, she called to the fox, who she felt was somehow responsible.

"Thank you," she called out.

And again, "Thanks."

Chapter Twenty-Three

she thought she might

have to search for days, but no, there he was, sitting beside the girl's chair in the field, almost as if he'd been waiting for her.

Together, the fox and the dog wove their way through backyards and under bushes. They darted across the road and wound their way to the creek, wading across, and then climbing the steep hill. At the top they stopped and looked over a meadow. In the distance, a man was riding a tall, golden-brown horse. As a rule, the fox kept her distance from larger animals, but the dog nodded his head in the horse's direction, and the fox followed him into the field.

"Wallace!" the man called out, and slowed the horse to a walk. "Where've you been?" He slipped off the horse, holding the reins in his right hand, and walked toward them. The fox looked around for a bush, a clump of weeds, anything to hide behind. But the field had been recently mown. Big bales of hay stood here and there, casting round shadows. The fox had nowhere to go, so she stayed where she was, standing perfectly still.

"Who you got there with you, boy?" the man asked, coming closer. "You find yourself a friend?"

And then he stopped. Opened his mouth, closed it again. Whispered, "A fox?" A grin broke out on his face, and he turned to the dog. "Wallace, you found yourself a fox. Probably the only one for twenty miles."

The man came even closer. He kneeled down to get a better look. The fox wanted to bolt, but one glance at the dog told her that would be a mistake.

"Look at you," the man said. "I'd say you

were a red fox, except you're a little more brown than red, and you're on the small side." He paused, thought for a moment. "Now, you couldn't be—*Vulpes velox*? A swift fox? No, no way. Not here. That's a prairie fox. A desert fox."

The fox took a step back. Her breath had become fast and shallow. The man's face, so close to her now, she knew it—she recognized this face. She saw it every night, saw it when she was up in the air, when she was falling into the flames, and the soldier beside her—

Was the man in front of her.

He looked older now. When she'd seen him in the sky, both of them thrown into the air by the explosion, he'd looked so much younger, barely grown. Now lines flared from the corners of his eyes.

How had he survived? They'd flown so high.

The fox's legs gave beneath her, and suddenly she found herself on the grass. She'd fallen from the sky into a field. And the soldier—this man— had fallen into a field too.

They were safe.

"I can't believe it." The soldier leaned forward to look in her face again. "I can't believe you made it."

The dog issued a brief bark, then turned and trotted back in the direction they'd come from. The fox lifted her face to the man. He laid his hand on top of her head, and then he let her go. She followed the dog back down the hill. When they reached the creek, the dog stopped, turned, looked at her. The fox waited for him to say something. Would she understand it? Did they share a language?

But the dog didn't speak. He nodded to the creek, and the fox knew it was time to cross back over, return to her field. On the other side, she stopped to shake the water off her fur. Turned to look back. The dog was still there.

He nodded once. *Stay close to her.*

And then he trotted back up the hill.

Chapter Twenty-Four

you're the first one here!" Kristen announced when she opened the Gorzcas' front door Friday night. "Why don't you go ahead and take your stuff to my room? Everybody else should be here soon."

Abby nodded and trudged up the stairs with her sleeping bag and backpack. *The only way out is through*, she told herself. She'd get this night over with and figure out a way to never have to do it again.

Kristen's room was at the end of the upstairs hallway. Right before school started, Mrs. Gorzca had painted large pink and brown polka dots on two of the walls, the ones without windows. Kristen's bedspread had the same design, and her curtains did too. Abby put her things down in front of the brown velveteen love seat across from Kristen's closet and sat down to get the full effect of all the dots. They were nice, she thought. Cheerful.

Then she noticed the small round table made of white plastic to the right of the love seat, next to the wall. A plate filled with Kit Kats, Snickers, and Reese's Cups—all of Abby's favorites—sat at its center, and Abby pondered whether or not to eat one. Her candy supply had run dangerously low, but ever since she'd been bitten by the fox, she hadn't wanted candy so much. Every once in a while, sure. But not every day. She hadn't thought of that until now. That was strange. Different.

She looked at the shiny wrappers. She'd had dreams like this, candy everywhere, and nobody to say no. There were so many, no one would notice if she took one. Besides, she could use some fortification. This was going to be a long, miserable night. She grabbed a Snickers bar from the plate and tore into it. She didn't want to be caught eating. Taking big bites, she chewed fast, then shoved the empty wrapper into her pocket.

She suddenly felt ravenous, as though she hadn't eaten for days. She shook a pair of Reese's Cups from their package and finished them off in four bites, then grabbed a Kit Kat and used her teeth to tear the paper.

As she split the candy bar in two, she heard somebody giggle. There was a rustling in Kristen's closet, and somebody else said, "Shh."

Abby went cold all over. Or hot. It was a weird sensation of freezing and burning up at the same time. The Kit Kat fell to the floor, and Abby looked at it. Maybe if she kept looking at it, this moment would stretch and stretch, until her whole life was just this moment of staring at the brown candy on the brown rug.

Another giggle came out of the closet.

"I know you're in there," Abby said flatly, picking up the Kit Kat bar from the floor. What should she do with it? Eat it? She wanted to eat it, but she knew she shouldn't. Not here. Not in front of them. She looked around for a trash can but didn't see one, so she put the candy back on the plate. "You can come out now."

Georgia and Rachel burst out of the closet, falling over each other. "Careful!" Rachel yelled. "You'll break the phone!"

"We got it! On video!" Georgia crowed to Abby, holding up a tiny cell phone. "We're going to post one of you pigging out on YouTube!"

So they finally figured out what to do, Abby thought. *Took them long enough.* She felt oddly calm, as though she no longer existed in her body, but floated outside of it. She noted that Myla, Bess, and Casey weren't here. Maybe they'd had enough, Abby thought. Maybe they were nice after all.

Kristen burst into the room. "Did you get it?" she squealed. Georgia held up the phone triumphantly. "Oh, my God! I can't believe it! That is so awesome!"

Abby stood up. "I'm going."

Kristen walked over and pushed her back down on the couch. "Oh, no you're not. What are you going to tell your mom? That you're a

210

little piggy? She'll put you on a diet before you have time to blink. And what will your dad say? We can send him the video as an e-mail attachment. I'm sure he'd get a big kick out of it."

Abby sat perfectly still. She felt trapped. Was trapped.

"We're going downstairs to eat pizza," Kristen informed her. "The candy bars are your dinner. We'll let you know when you can come out."

The girls left the room, laughing and pushing into one another. Abby stared straight ahead. She breathed in deeply through her nose. She thought about her starfish collection.

She started to cry anyway.

Stop it, she told herself. *Just stop*. But she couldn't stop. She thought everything had changed, but nothing had. She wasn't different at all. She was still a girl who stuffed herself with candy bars, a girl everyone else laughed at. Nothing new about that. Stupid, fat Abby stuffing her mouth. No wonder people hated her. She deserved it.

Stop it.

Abby spun around. Who said that? She walked over to the closet and looked in. Empty except for Kristen's clothes and shoes and two tennis rackets. She went to the window and looked out. There, in a patch of silvery moonlight, stood the fox.

So she hadn't imagined the fox after all. She opened the window. "What should I do?" she called out, and the fox looked at her with what seemed to Abby sympathetic eyes.

The wind answered with a sudden rustling of leaves. A crow answered with a loud *caw, caw*. The fox looked at her for a long moment, as if waiting for Abby to answer her own question.

Abby nodded. "Okay."

The fox slipped into the shadows. Abby closed the window.

She grabbed her sleeping bag and backpack from the floor in front of the love seat. She thought about grabbing the rest of the candy from the plate, but she didn't really want it now. She went down the stairs, opened the front door, and left without saying good-bye.

"Where are you going?" Kristen yelled after her from the front door as Abby trundled down the driveway. All the medium girls leaked out of the house and onto the sidewalk. "You can't go home! We'll send that video to your dad!"

Abby stopped. She put her bags down on the driveway and turned around. "And then you'll have to explain it to *your* mom—and my mom, for that matter, won't you? What you were doing making a video of me like that. You'd be doing me a favor. My mom thinks you're my friend."

"Well, your dad's going to think you're a fat pig!" Kristen shrieked.

"I'll just have to live with that," Abby told her. She picked her bags back up and headed toward the street.

It was two weeks until Halloween. A few weeks after that it would be winter, and the birds would fly south. Would the fox go south too? Abby didn't think that animals other than birds migrated, but the fox was so small and delicate, it seemed too fragile for winter. Where would it find food?

Abby stopped. She stood in front of the yard

213

across the street from her house and stared. There was a sign. How had she not noticed the sign? She'd been too upset, she supposed, about having to go to the sleepover. That would be the only way to explain how she'd missed the FOR SALE sign where the mailbox once stood.

For sale. If she had money, she'd buy the lot, and she'd live there. She imagined living in her chair by the oak tree, the red cooler by her side filled with grapes. She could spread a tarp over the tree branches when it rained and drag out the old beach umbrella from the garage on superhot days, for extra shade. But what would she do about going to the bathroom? Abby snorted. What a life. She crossed the street to go home. She thought when she got inside she might call Marlys and tell her what happened. Would Marlys laugh when Abby told her about how she ate that candy like a starving person?

No, Abby knew that she wouldn't. Marlys wasn't against anyone, especially not Abby.

Abby crossed the street to her house and ran up the stairs to the front porch. She had the helium feeling again, the dance-around-in-circles feeling. The world was a new and undiscovered place, filled with horses and foxes and prong-horn deer. And friends. Friends along for the expedition.

Chapter Twenty-Five

november. abby

sat in her chair behind the oak, knowing that without the weeds, she wasn't so hidden anymore. She looked around her. She couldn't believe the weeds were gone. And the flowers. Even the robins had flown away. When they came back next spring, would there be a new house standing here?

She pulled her sweater tighter. It was getting cold.

A car door slammed twenty feet away, and Anoop's voice called out, "Abby, are you there?"

She turned to see him standing at the edge of the lot, peering around. When he saw her, his face brightened. "There you are! You are hidden behind the trees!"

"Well, not so hidden that you didn't see me," Abby said, getting up from her chair. "Did you wear sneakers, like I told you?"

Anoop walked toward her. He was dressed in jeans and a heavy sweater, a ski cap pulled down over his ears. "My athletic shoes are only for PE. But I have hiking boots that I got for summer camp last summer." He stuck out his leg and pointed to his foot. "See?"

"Your grandmother let you go to summer camp?"

"We told her it was computer camp," Anoop said with a shrug. "We did not mention the rock-climbing aspect."

Abby folded her chair and leaned it against the tree. "Did you bring the poem?"

Anoop held out a manila envelope. "Yes. It is typed. I now owe my sister two weeks of dish washing."

"Two weeks? Boy!" Abby wondered if that was a high price for twenty pages' worth of poetry? Twenty pages was a lot, but poems were skinny. "I could come over and help, at least on weekends."

Anoop shook his head. "For our dishwasher, you don't even have to rinse the dishes. It is all very easy."

They walked to the fence at the back of the lot. "Are they still getting the horse today?" Anoop asked as they climbed over. "I am eager to see the new horse. My great-grandfather was from Marwar, and he rode a great Marwari stallion. This is according to my grandmother. She is telling me everything about our family's history, so that I won't forget."

"Did you tell her about seeing the horses today?"

"You are kidding," Anoop said. "Or else you are quite mad."

Wallace was waiting for them on the sidewalk. "That dog looks as if he is expecting us," Anoop observed.

"He is," Abby said.

They ambled down the path to the creek. Anders was waiting for them, on their side of the water. The week before, Abby had gone to the creek and there he'd been, sitting on a rock, like it wasn't a big deal that he crossed on his own. "We decided it was time to expand the safe perimeters," Anders had explained. "Matt said it was okay for me to come across if I wanted to."

That was the day Matt had left for the VA hospital. "A room finally opened up," Mrs. Benton had told Abby when she and Anders reached the farmhouse. Her eyes were red, but there was something softer about her, Abby thought, like maybe now she didn't have to be so strong all the time.

"How long will he be gone?" Abby had asked. She was glad Matt was going to get the help he needed, but she wanted him to be there to watch her ride Ruckus, too. To help her get better at it.

"His doctor at the VA says it'll probably be at least two months. It's a good hospital. It's good for Matt to be around other soldiers who've been through the same thing."

"He's going to call us every night," Anders reported. "He wants to stay up to speed on how the horses are doing. He wants us to all be on the same page."

Now Abby looked at Anders and said, "Your feet are soaked."

"I jumped," Anders explained. "But I guess I didn't jump far enough."

"Will it be your horse?" Anoop asked Anders as the three of them ran after Wallace up the hill toward the farm. "The new one, I mean."

"No, I get Ruckus," Anders said. "The new horse is Matt's, for when he gets back. Grandma sold the Virginia Highlander, the one that was always biting, so that we could afford it."

Abby slowed halfway up the hill, holding her side. Anders kept running, but Anoop slowed with her, trotting beside her.

"It is quite a serious hill," he said, panting a little bit.

"It's not so bad," Abby panted back. "You get used to it. After a while you hardly notice."

And then she took off and ran as fast as she

could, Anoop laughing behind her, trying to catch up.

"Hey, there!" Mrs. Benton waved at them from across the field as they came over the hill. "Come see!" she called from the paddock.

The horse had a mottled gray-and-white coat and stood a good hand taller than Ruckus. "Meet Shannon," Mrs. Benton said. "She's a beauty, don't you think? An Appaloosa."

Abby slowly approached the horse and reached out her hand, palm up, flat. "Hello, Shannon," she said, feeling a little shaky next to such a big animal. "Nice horse."

Shannon put her nose in Abby's hand. It was velvet soft. She sniffed, and Abby laughed.

"Matt wants you to ride her until he gets home," Mrs. Benton told her. "Exercise her every afternoon if you can."

"I don't know," Abby said, her heart fluttering. "I haven't had very much practice at it yet."

"He says you know what you're doing. I'll give you some lessons, show you how to put on a saddle." Mrs. Benton grinned. "You can pay me back by helping Anders muck the stalls."

Abby relaxed. "I can help muck," she said, confident about that at least. "I like how the barn smells."

"Like perfume," Anders said.

"They should bottle it," Abby agreed.

Anoop was still holding the envelope with the typed poem. "Shall we leave this with you, Mrs. Benton, or mail it to Anders's father at the hospital? He will want to see how his poem looks printed out. My sister used a special font. It looks quite regal."

"I'll bring it when Anders and I go visit Matt tomorrow," Mrs. Benton said, reaching out her hand to take the envelope from Anoop. "He says his doctor wants to read it."

"Especially the part about the fox," Anders added. "Dr. Reynolds is very interested in the part about the fox."

Abby turned to Anoop. "You want to learn how to muck a stall? It's kind of fun."

Anoop looked doubtful. "I suppose. But if I go home smelling like horse manure, my grandmother will be suspicious."

They stayed at the barn for a couple of hours, cleaning out the stalls and talking about horses, which kinds were the fastest, which were the best for riding through the countryside. Anders dreamed of owning a quarter horse one day, or a golden palomino, and Abby thought she might like to ride a Belgian draft horse, the biggest horse of all. "When I get brave enough," she added, crossing her fingers that one day she would have that kind of courage.

"You have heard of jodhpurs?" Anoop asked, leaning against his shovel, and when Abby and Anders nodded, he continued, "The great Marwari stallion is from the Jodhpur region of India. It is the most spirited horse in the world. Do you know that Marwari stallions performed at my grandmother's wedding? She says they wore diamond bridles."

"Pretty fancy," Anders said admiringly. "I'd like to see that."

"It is rather amazing," Anoop said, sounding rather amazed himself. "I have seen the pictures."

Abby and Anoop left at twenty minutes before

five so that Anoop would be back at Abby's in time to be picked up by his mother.

"It is good to be around horses," Anoop declared after they'd jumped over the creek on the way back. "Maybe I should bring my grandmother sometime. The horses might make her remember when she was young, and life was not so frightening."

Abby stayed in the lot after Anoop's mother picked him up. She set out her chair again and sat down, even though she knew she needed to get home. It made her mother unhappy when Abby was late. Abby still didn't like making her mother unhappy, though now she knew that sometimes she had to.

That night. Coming back home with her sleeping bag and backpack. Her mother had paled when Abby told her what had happened, the candy, the cell phone, what the girls planned to do. Her mother hadn't said much, just that she was sorry. They could talk it all over with Abby's father in the morning.

Abby knew they wouldn't.

The next Monday, Abby sat at her usual spot

in the cafeteria with Anoop and Jafar. There had been only three girls at the medium girls' table: Kristen, Georgia, and Rachel. Abby scanned the room until she found the others—Bess and Myla were sitting at a table over by the back window with two girls Abby didn't know, and Casey was eating by herself, reading. Kristen, Georgia, and Rachel leaned over their lunches, talking in whispers as their eyes darted around the cafeteria. What were they plotting now? Abby wondered. How long before Rachel wandered off to find another friend, and it was just Kristen and Georgia at a table by themselves, looking around for someone else to make miserable?

When would they figure out they were the miserable ones?

A few stars blinked in the darkening sky. Abby thought about riding Shannon. It scared her, imagining sitting up so high. It would take getting used to. Maybe she'd fall. Crack a collarbone. Break her neck.

Abby laughed. Maybe she'd get run over crossing the street to go home for dinner. The possibilities of what might happen to her were endless. She stood and picked up the cooler. She left the chair. Someday someone would buy the wild lot, build a new house on it, make it the same as every other place. The weeds would fly off and land somewhere else. The fox would move on.

But until that day, this place was hers.

Chapter Twenty-Six

the fox tried to tell Crow the story, but Crow refused to believe her.

You flew? Crow asked, sounding doubtful. *You flew up into the air, flew over the desert, and landed here?*

The fox looked around her. She had to admit the field didn't look like much. It was a different place now, here in the first days of winter. Most of the weeds were gone. All that was left were clumps of brown grass stirring in the chilly breeze. No flowers, no birds. The trees remained, but their branches were bare.

Well. Crow sniffed. *Not much to look at. Let's move on.*

The fox nodded. *Time to find a new story.*

Crow flew above her as the fox began to trot in the direction of the creek. *My natural habitat is the prairie,* she bragged to Crow. *Wide fields, big skies.*

My natural habitat is in dreams, Crow retorted. *In every mind, in every eye, Crow flies.*

The fox snorted. *You sound like a raccoon, the way you spout nonsense.*

Crow took to the sky. *Let's see how you fly, Fox! Let's see you sprout wings.*

Who needs wings? the fox thought, and she began to run, the wind brushing back her fur, her paws thudding against the hard clay dirt. She closed her eyes. She leaped into the invisible air.

Acknowledgments

The author would like to thank Caitlyn M. Dlouhy, who makes everything so much better, and Ariel Colletti, for batting cleanup. Thanks also to Justin Chanda for his unflagging support, and Kaitlin Severini for her copyediting eagle eye. The author owes a huge debt of gratitude to Jennifer Gardner at Prettyfab PR, and sends big hugs to her homegirls, Amy Graham, Danielle Paul, and Sarah Schulz, for *their* ongoing support. Thanks to Virginia Hall, fifth-grade history teacher extraordinaire, who got her family all excited about the Lewis and Clark expedition, and thanks, too, to poet Campbell McGrath—

not only for his book *Shannon*, but for all his books, from *Capitalism* on, which have made this writer's world a better place to be in. Finally, she is full of love and wonder when she thinks about those boys she lives with, Clifton, Jack, Will, and Travis the dog, i.e. the Dowells, otherwise known as her own ones.